CARNIVOROUS LUNAR ACTIVITIES

MAX BOOTH III

FANGORIA.COM
@FANGORIA
DALLAS, TX

"Booth's book is a breakthrough, from the conceit to the delivery. It's funny but mean, smart but smartass, and it just might be your favorite werewolf story in the world.

Carnivorous Lunar Activities starts out like a play, Grand Guignol, a couple of very compelling characters locked in a helluva conversation, before transforming into a blood-bright explosion of horror joy.

Fucked up love, fucked up friendship, and how maybe you shouldn't live past the best night of your life. Oh, how I loved this book."

—Josh Malerman, author of *Bird Box*

"What I like about Max's point of view is when he looks at something familiar - something you or I might have seen dozens of times and not give a second thought to - he comes up with a whole new way of seeing it, in the process causing you to reconsider your own perspective. That fresh pair of eyes is on grand display in *Carnivorous Lunar Activities*."

—Phil Nobile Jr., Editor-in-Chief of *FANGORIA*

"This book is a fucking blood-thirsty joy and if it's not made into a movie in the next couple of years, I'll eat my hat. Luckily, I don't own any hats, but you get the idea. It's about two friends. One happens to be chained to an anchor in his own basement – yes, an anchor – and he's a werewolf. The other guy has got a whole other set of problems. There's another Max walking around out there with the last name, but Max Booth is the literary inheritor of John Landis's mantle and *Carnivorous Lunar Activities* could be the sequel to the comic-tragedy of *An American Werewolf in London*. This werewolf romp is a howling good time. (Sorry, couldn't help myself.)"

> —John Hornor Jacobs, author of
> *A Lush and Seething Hell*

"*Carnivorous Lunar Activities* is laugh-out-loud funny with dialogue that'll make even the most seasoned writers jealous. Joe R. Lansdale meets *An American Werewolf in London* with a splash of Michael Haneke's *Funny Games*. *Carnivorous Lunar Activities* is a must for all horror fans."

—Michael David Wilson, *This is Horror* Founder

"Fun and ridiculously propulsive, a chatty, earthy, lived-in horror for fans of Landis and Lansdale."

> —Meredith Borders, Managing Editor
> of *FANGORIA*

*This book is dedicated to anyone who
would be willing to kill me.*

"*Everything makes sense if you look at it long enough.*"
—Stephen Graham Jones, *Mongrels*

"*Have you ever tried talking to a corpse? It's boring!*"
—Jack, *An American Werewolf in London*

PART 1

POST MERIDIEM

ONE

TED WAS THINKING ABOUT KILLING HIS WIFE WHEN his cell phone rang.

He heard the ringing but it didn't sound real. The car had been quiet for so long, any intrusions felt false. Make-believe. He was lost in a trance, vision glued to his mother-in-law's house, a red bricked bungalow protected by a white fence and an assortment of various shrubberies. He sat in his car with the engine off, an October breeze slipping in through the rolled-down windows. He'd parked at the mouth of the cul-de-sac out of fear of either Shelly or her mom calling the cops if they spotted him. He searched for any sign of Shelly inside her mom's house, maybe walking past a window or exiting through the front door. He bit his lip and dug his nails into his palms, consumed with ugly thoughts he didn't like but couldn't do anything about, either.

A man couldn't just stop thinking something just because it was wrong. He wasn't a machine. The only shut-off switch came in the form of a bullet to the brain, which he figured would follow once he'd taken care of Shelly. Jesus Christ. What kind of talk was that? Ted wasn't a killer. He loved his wife. Loved her more than anything in the whole goddamn world. But he couldn't see a future without her and she couldn't see one with him so what other choice did that leave him?

He hadn't slept in a very long time.

Maybe his phone had been ringing for a couple seconds or maybe a couple hours. Maybe he'd already glanced at the phone and erased it from his memory when he saw it wasn't Shelly. Now he looked down at the phone again for either the first time or second or third or fourth and the name on the screen said JUSTIN but that didn't make any sense, so he blinked long and hard and when he read it again it still said the same thing, so he answered it because what the hell.

"Justin?"

"Holy shit, dude, I was beginning to think I had the wrong number or something." He laughed, but he didn't sound amused—more overwhelmed with a sort of panic or desperation than anything.

"You okay? What's going on?"

"What? Can't a guy call up his best friend and shoot the shit once in a while?"

"We haven't talked in like three years." Ted leaned back in his seat, desperately wanting to close his eyes and take a nap but afraid he'd miss sight of Shelly.

"And that's a goddamn shame, don't you think?"

"Sure."

"So, yeah, I was just sitting here at the crib, knocking back a couple cold ones, you know how it goes, and I got to thinking maybe it'd be a good idea if you came on over and hung out with me for a few. Got some stuff I need to talk to you about, anyway. Things that need to be said.

"Yeah, okay. Maybe I can get out there sometime next

week." Truth be told, Ted had no real intention of meeting up with him, or anybody else for that matter. They could make plans for whatever day Justin wanted, but Ted would not be showing up. He doubted he'd even live through the night. Not the way life was looking. He failed to see a point in it. He thought about the rifle Shelly's father kept in his study back when he was still alive and wondered if it was still there or if Shelly's mom threw it out. How fast could he get to it? How fast could a man's mind complete-ly deteriorate? How loud could his wife scream? None of these questions were logical but he couldn't stop them from overflowing his thoughts. Like a burst dam flooding a city. Help would not arrive fast enough to prevent some casualties.

Justin cleared his throat, struggling not to choke on phlegm. "How about now?"

"No."

"Why not?"

"I can't. Sorry. I'm—I'm really busy."

Ted glared at his mother-in-law's house, prepared to remain parked out here for the rest of his life. Nothing else mattered at this point. He needed to see her. And if she didn't want to see him, then he didn't know, maybe she didn't deserve to see anything else ever again. Sure, that wasn't exactly fair, but a lot of things weren't fair these days, were they? He'd never imagined harming Shelly in a mil-lion years. He loved her with every ounce of him. They'd been together since they were kids. So Ted had made a mistake. One *goddamn* mistake. That didn't mean things had to end. That didn't mean the life they'd built together had to be over. It wasn't fucking fair.

"Oh, come on, man. You ain't doin' shit. Come over.

Drink some beers. Let's catch up. Now's as good a time as any."

"Maybe next weekend, okay?"

"No." Justin coughed loud and violent and Ted jerked away from the phone as if Justin's spit could somehow eject from one device to the other. "Listen. There's some stuff we gotta discuss, all right? I can't put it off any longer. This shit needs to happen today. Now."

"What are you talking about? What stuff?" He considered just ending the call. He didn't give a shit about any of this. He needed to talk to Shelly. He needed her to give him a reason not to do the things he felt like doing.

"Stuff I can't talk about over the phone, okay? I…trust me, dude, something like this, it's…better discussed in person."

"I'm sorry, but it's going to have to wait."

"Man, fuck you, Teddy. This. Can't. Wait. Ain't you listening? What, you think I'd just call you up out of the blue if this shit wasn't an emergency? We're talking life or death here, dude. Life or motherfucking death."

As Justin spoke, the front door of the house opened and Ted's mother-in-law stepped out onto the porch, wearing a robe and smoking a cigarette. Goddamn woman was hiding his wife from him. She honestly thought he wouldn't walk right on in there if he wanted to. She thought he was afraid of her. Fuck the both of them. Ted would knock that old bitch off the porch and barge inside and track down his wife and demand a conversation between the two of them, that's all he really wanted, just a goddamn conversation. It was the silence that was driving him crazy. The goddamn nothingness.

Life or death.

Ted sighed and at last closed his eyes, realizing how close he'd just come to becoming a monster. He told Justin he was on the way, and Justin asked if he could pick him up some burgers.

"I'm fuckin' starving, dude."

TWO

HE HADN'T DRIVEN OUT TO HAMMOND SINCE Justin's mother's funeral. It wasn't that long of a drive from Percy, maybe forty-five minutes with traffic, tops. The place was just depressing as hell, was the thing. Most cities, they expand and adapt with the future. Hammond, though…if it wasn't stagnant, it was an anchor. It'd been a shit-hole when Ted lived there as a kid and it was still a shit-hole as he drove through it now. Shops and businesses abandoned and burned. Windows constructed more of cardboard and wood than glass. Shopping carts overflowing with empty cans and discarded knickknacks, pushed by vagabonds cocooned in layers of mud and ash.

Nothing had ever felt more like home.

He stopped at a McDonald's and ordered some food in the drive-thru. He checked his phone as he waited. Still no word from Shelly. He hadn't expected anything to change but that didn't mean his hope had been snuffed. He sent her another text message that read: "You mean everything to me."

He stared at the screen hallucinating all the possible responses she could send until the drive-thru cashier sighed. "Mister, are you gonna take your food or not?"

He apologized and she rolled her eyes and told him he was holding up the line so he grabbed the bag and drinks and drove away before she could yell at him some more. He stopped in the parking lot of the McDonald's and picked up his phone again. Still no response. This time he called her. It rang seven or eight times then gave in to the robot. He left a message. He couldn't remember how many he'd recorded since she left.

"Goddammit, Shelly, I'm sorry, don't you know that? I'm sorry. Just call me back, okay? Just fucking talk to me. Can't you do that? Can't you just do that?"

Ted threw the phone on the floor of the passenger's side and cried and drove. He reached in the McDonald's bag next to him and shoveled a handful of hot fries down his throat, but it didn't seem to help him stop crying.

He turned off the main street and drove a couple blocks, then wheeled into an alley and parked behind the fourth house on the right.

209 Gostlin.

The phone started ringing from the car floor and he had to unbuckle his seat belt to reach it. Not Shelly, but Justin.

"What?"

"Dude, where the fuck are you?"

"I'm here."

"Then what are you waiting for?"

"Just give me a second. Shit."

"You're underestimating the worth of a second."

Whatever the hell that meant.

Ted scrunched his face at the phone and pressed END CALL and stuffed it in his pants pocket, resisting the urge to redial Shelly a thousand more times.

The house hadn't changed much since they were boys. Discolored paint chips surrounded the structure like skin-shavings. An antenna hung off the side of the roof, the wind forcing it to dance with a cracked rain gutter. Black circles and faded paint splotches ran along ancient hardiplank and brought back memories of rogue roman candles and paintball gun fights. The house had seemed so much bigger and indestructible back then.

Ted had to set down the bags of fast food along with the accompanying fountain drinks on the gravel driveway and use both hands to pull up the fence's latch in the back yard. A sharp screech shot through the alley as he pushed the gate open. Twenty years ago, this fence hadn't exactly looked brand new, but at least you could tell it was silver. Now, you'd think the thing had been painted brown from the get-go.

He double-checked his car was locked before retrieving the fast food from the ground and heading into the back yard. He'd grown up in this neighborhood. Not this house specifically, but close. He knew what happened to cars you left unlocked here. Hell, twenty—even ten—years ago, he would have been the one searching for the unlocked car.

Grass threatened to swallow his feet as he approached the back door. Ants and other curious insects stared up at him from their jungle, contemplating the motives of a giant. The door was ajar and the knob was missing. Something had dented the frame, reminded him of how doors looked in movies after someone's kicked it open.

Ted hadn't been here since Justin's parents died, but that didn't stop him from entering without knocking. This place had practically been a second home, growing up. He didn't think he'd ever knocked on this door in his life.

He wasn't about to start now.

THREE

HE MADE IT ONE STEP INSIDE THE HOUSE BEFORE the smell assaulted him full-force. Like mold and rotten meat and cat piss all mixed together. A stench so powerful it knocked his head back, practically told him his only choice was to turn around and pretend like Justin never called begging for his help. Maybe go back to Shelly's mom's house and beg forgiveness, try to convince her that he'd never be a shithead again, if only he was given a second chance, a third chance, a fourth—if only he could make it all better.

"Teddy? That you, dude?"

Too late now. But who was Ted kidding? It'd been too late the moment he answered his cell phone.

He stood inside the house, next to the still-opened back door. Directly ahead, a framed photograph of Justin as a child stared at him. Eight-year-old Justin held a baseball bat and wore the cheesiest grin a kid ever owned. Probably around the same year Ted and he had become friends. They'd been on the same Little League team, practiced together every weekend up the street at Hermit Park, trying their damnedest to crack a ball over the yellow fence top protector straight down center field and never once succeeding.

To his left, he could continue down the steps into the basement. Ted instead turned right and walked upstairs to the kitchen. Slow, deliberate steps, predicting which ones would creak from memory. Things he and Justin had to learn when they were stoned teenagers craving junk food at two in the morning.

Justin leaned against the counter, in the process of gulping down a beer. He waved at Ted and Ted just stood in place, unable to move from the top of the staircase. Justin had never been fat or anything, but he'd never been skinny, either. Looking at him now, even "skinny" couldn't justly define what Ted was seeing. Malnourished, maybe. Pale like the dead except for around his eyes, which seemed sunken with darkness. He'd always kept his hair cut short, but now it shagged down to his shoulders. He'd also grown the kind of beard that would've guaranteed any potential employer to throw his job application in the trash. The Manson Family, however, would have welcomed him with open arms.

"Justin…"

He tossed the now-empty can in the sink and stepped toward him. "You came."

"Holy shit."

"Before you even say anything, I already know I look like a fuckin' nutjob."

"You look like shit, man."

He tossed up his hands and rolled his eyes and looked from side to side as if fishing for moral support from an audience of ghosts. "Jesus Christ, I just said I knew that, didn't I?"

"What—what's wrong? What's going on?"

Justin eyed the McDonald's. "You got the food."

"Yeah."

"Thank Christ." He licked his lips.

"Justin—"

He held up his hand, palm out, and closed his eyes. He looked like he hadn't slept in years. "Before we get into it, I...I need to eat. I'm so fucking hungry, dude, you have no idea."

"When was the last time you've eaten?"

"Uh." He scratched the infected hives spread out across his face. "What time is it?"

"Like one. Almost two."

"Shit. What took you so long? It feels like it's been days since I called you."

"It's only been an hour. At most."

"Oh."

"Justin—"

"Food? Please?"

"Okay, okay."

They sat at the kitchen table. Ted placed the food and drinks down and Justin tore a vertical slit through the side of the bag.

Ted pointed at the ripped remains. "You know, there's an opening at the top you could've just reached into."

"Don't got time for that kinda bullshit."

"Oh-kay…"

He snagged one of the burgers and pried it from its wrapping and bit into it. His eyes rolled into the back of his skull as he moaned.

"Oh, hell yes. Fuck yes. This is the shit, my man. This is the motherfuckin' shit, right here."

"Justin, what—what the hell is—"

Justin's orgasmic expression spiraled into a grimace and he looked at the half-eaten burger with disgust. "Goddammit. I thought I said no pickles."

"I told them no pickles."

"Maybe I got yours instead."

"Maybe."

He dropped the burger on the table and grabbed Ted's unopened one. He tore the wrapping off and flipped the bun over and dug his fingers through the condiments. His nails were black and ragged beyond expiration. "No, this one's got pickles too."

"I'm sorry."

"Ugh. I swear, I could turn into the goddamn swamp monster and I'd still hate pickles." He paused and breathed deeply and shrugged and devoured the rest of his burger. "Hey, I'm gonna eat yours, too. I'm sorry. I need it. Just let me have it. Okay? Please."

"It's fine. Go ahead."

"You're a real trooper, Teddy."

"When was the last time you've eaten?"

"I don't know."

"You don't know?"

"Maybe twenty minutes ago? Twenty days? Who knows? It's hard sometimes, keeping track. Every meal is just...like, one big meal, and it never ends, you know? Food is life." He belched. "The moment you run out, you cease to exist."

"What the hell are you talking about?"

"Wait, did you only bring the two burgers?"

"Yeah…"

"I told you, we'd need more than this."

"No, you didn't."

"I said to bring a shit-ton of food."

"I figured two burgers and fries would be enough for both of us. You didn't—"

"Man, fuck these fries." He knocked the fries off the table and they scattered across the floor. "Who the fuck gives a shit about fries? I need *meat*, Teddy. Where's the fucking *meat*?"

"You're eating it."

"I need more."

"You don't have anything here?"

Justin laughed but Ted didn't understand the joke. "Anything here that was worth a damn is long, long gone."

"Haven't you gone grocery shopping?"

He shook his head and glanced at the window above the sink. "I prefer not to leave the house."

"Why?"

He tapped his bruised, swollen knuckles against the table and closed his eyes again. "Terrible things seem to keep happening when I'm outside."

"What does that mean?"

"It means maybe lions are better off locked up."

"Uh…what?"

"Although sometimes that still ain't enough to protect 'em. Sometimes you just gotta put 'em down once and for all."

"I think I need to take you to the hospital, man. Something…something's wrong with you."

He opened his eyes, wide and psychotic. "Nothing's fucking wrong with me."

He punched the table and it shook hard enough to knock over the fountain drinks. Coke splashed down to the floor and dragged the fallen french fries across the linoleum like drowning victims. Ted jumped up to gather paper towels but the paper towel holder was empty, so he used a couple of old dish rags discarded next to the sink. Moldy dishes and empty beer cans filled the basin. An entire planet for maggots and flies to make their home.

Justin rocked back and forth in his chair, breathing in and out, in and out. "Okay, so something's wrong with me. I can acknowledge that. Sure. But nothing that some goddamn hospital can fix. At least, I don't think so. That's what we're going to find out, right?"

Still on his hands and knees, Ted looked up from the mess. "What?"

"Okay, so here's the thing. I called you here for a reason."

"And that would be…?"

"I'm sick."

Ted nodded like *no shit.* "It's okay, man, I know."

"No, you don't fuckin' *know,* all right? You got no fuckin' *idea.*"

Ted got off the floor and dropped the wet rags into the sink, on top of a mountain of empty beer cans. "Then tell me. I'm here. I'm listening. It's okay."

He laughed. "It ain't okay, bro. It ain't okay at all."

"Whatever's wrong, you'll get the help you need. I'm here for you." The words left his mouth, but they felt cold and robotic. It was hard to give a shit about whatever drama Justin had gotten himself mixed up in this time. Ted debated turning around and driving back to Shelly's house. His phone burned in his pocket and he feared it would soon eat through his skin. He sat at the table. "We've been friends how long? You can trust me."

"Well, Teddy, I do appreciate that. Because I definitely need your help."

"Anything."

He reached behind his back and pulled out a black revolver, then laid it on the kitchen table between them. "Tonight, at midnight, I'm gonna need you to shoot me in the heart."

FOUR

TED HAD SCREWED UP. SHOULD'VE NEVER ANSWERED his goddamn phone. Should've never fucking come here.

"I'm sorry, but I gotta go." He stood and tried to turn around toward the stairs, but Justin picked up the revolver and pointed it at him. But he didn't look very threatening. More pathetic than anything.

"Please sit down."

"Are you—"

"Don't make me do anything I don't wanna do, okay? Just…just sit down." He waved the barrel toward the empty chair. "These bullets ain't meant for you, anyway."

Slowly he returned to the table, eyes moving from Justin's desolate expression to the eternal void breathing within the revolver's barrel. "Where'd you get the gun from?"

"The hell you think? The gun store."

"Okay." He tried imagining Justin walking into a store and buying a firearm and the whole thing seemed laughable, even with him holding one now. "And, uh…why did you buy a gun?"

"Because I need killing, and knowin' me, I'd only fuck it up."

"What do you mean, you need killing?"

"I need to die."

"Justin. Come on, man. Is this about your parents? What's going on? Why do you want to kill yourself?"

"I didn't say I *want* to kill myself, did I? I said I *need* to. It ain't my call. Sometimes things just need to be done and there's no side-stepping around it and this here is one of 'em."

"You're not making any sense."

"I know that's what you—hey, I said to sit the fuck down."

"I...I *am* sitting."

"Yeah, but you was considerin' otherwise."

"I...I don't—"

He tapped the barrel of the revolver against his temple. "I don't see the same way normal people do. You and me, we're different. Me, I...I can see. I can really *see*. Not just the bullshit in front of me, but...but through the layers."

"The layers."

"Yeah. The layers. Like you look at an onion, right, and you peel it, but you ain't reached the end yet, have you? There's layers. That's the universe, Teddy. A series of layers. And me? I can see through them all."

"And what is it you see?"

He paused and scratched the side of his head with the revolver. Dandruff drifted from his skull and disintegrated in front of him. "I see the end."

"Because the universe is an onion."

"Dude. It was a fuckin' metaphor. Or a simile. Or what-ever the fuck. You get it."

Ted shrugged, although it felt awkward and forced. "I always liked the smell of onions."

"That's because you're a goddamn freak."

Ted started to laugh then saw the gun again and his face sagged. "I'm not going to shoot you."

"You haven't even heard me out yet."

"There's nothing you could possibly say that'd convince me to do it."

"You don't even want to know, huh?"

"No. I do. I just would prefer you tell me all about it as I drive you to the hospital."

He set the revolver down on the table and covered his face with his hands and groaned. He waited a beat and removed them and stared at Teddy matter-of-factly. "If you take me to the hospital, there's a real good goddamn chance everybody there will die."

"What? That—that doesn't make any—how—*why* would they die?"

"I'd kill 'em all."

"But...but why?"

He held up both hands, empty of answers. "Why do dogs chase squirrels?"

"Wh-what?"

"There's something in me, Teddy. I've done changed. I'm not the same kid you grew up with."

"You're just not well is all. If you got some help…"

"Goddammit, ain't you listening?" He slammed his fist against the table and the revolver did a little bounce. "*You're* my help. There ain't nobody else around more qualified."

"Shooting you isn't helping you."

"I think you'd disagree if you was in my shoes."

"So put me in your shoes."

Justin chuckled. "The kinda shoes I got, Teddy, once you put 'em on, there ain't no takin' 'em off."

"Try me."

He scratched his beard and dug some kind of food out from deep inside the hairs and threw it in his mouth and swallowed it without chewing. "Two thousand."

"Two thousand?"

"Or twenty-oh-oh. Shit, however the fuck you're supposed to say it, I don't know. The year. Two thousand. The new century."

"What about two thousand?"

"How old were we, you reckon?"

"Uh. I don't know. Like fifteen?"

"Fourteen."

"Okay, sure. What about it?"

"That was a great summer, wasn't it?"

"I don't really remember any significant details, to be honest."

"Well, *I* do. *I* remember."

"Did...did something happen?"

"You bet your luscious ass something happened. Two thousand. *July*, two thousand, to be more specific. Afraid I don't recall the exact date any longer, but it was definitely a Saturday. Saturday night at fourteen, here in the basement,"—he pointed to the floor—"below this very kitchen."

"We spent a lot of nights down there. It was like a tiny apartment just for us."

"Yeah, but not many of those nights did we have the place to ourselves. My folks were always creaking down the steps, trying to spy on us and shit. But sometimes— sometimes they went out, and it was just us. For the whole night."

"Oh."

"Memories suddenly come flooding back, huh?"

"Something like that."

"A grown man blushing sure is an interesting sight."

"I'm not blushing." Instinct brought his hand to his face.

"Your face is redder than your innards."

"Maybe it is."

"Let's go down and take a look."

"What, the basement?"

"Yeah, why not? This kitchen's fuckin' useless now, anyway." He shook his head, still pissed off, and stood from the table. He picked up the revolver. "Only two burgers. What the fuck."

"You gonna put that gun down?"

"All in due time, brother."

FIVE

THE BASEMENT SMELLED LIKE SOMETHING HAD SPOILED. Either Justin had gotten used to it by now, or he just didn't give a shit. He grinned and spread out his arms and did a little twirl like a realtor putting on a show. "Flashback heaven or what?"

"I don't remember heaven smelling so bad."

He slumped his shoulders like Ted had killed his spirit. "Maybe I'm a bit behind on the laundry."

"Was your mom still doing it for you, before she passed?"

"You know, for the one guy here without a gun, you're kind of a dick."

Ted smiled for the first time in a week. "Yeah?"

"Yeah."

"I guess being down here again...you're right, it brings back memories. We used to rag on each other all the time."

Justin nodded, one hand in his pocket and the other awkwardly twirling the revolver. He coughed and something red and wet flew from his mouth. "Remember that time you and Bobby slept over? What we did?"

"You're gonna have to be a little more specific."

"Specific?"

"Yeah."

"Okay." He licked his lips, savoring the memory. "We jacked off in tissues and rubbed our cum all over his palm, then tickled his face with a feather."

"Oh Jesus Christ." Ted gagged. "I forgot all about that. Oh my god."

"Then, because we had tickled him, he tried scratching his face with the hand we had covered with our cum, only to end up getting cum all over his face and he started going, 'Oh god, what's on me? What's on me?' And we said, 'That's our cum, Bobby. You got our cum on you.'"

"Okay, please stop."

"You told me to be specific."

Ted tried holding back a laugh. "That's fucking awful. I can't believe we did that."

"Yet you're still laughing."

"So are you."

"Well, that's because it's funny."

"Shit. Goddamn. We should be on some sort of sex offenders' list."

"Yet, out of the three of us, he was the one who ended up having to register."

"Ha."

"His life is pretty much ruined at this point."

Ted stopped laughing. "Wait, are you serious?"

"Uh, yeah, dude. You didn't hear?"

"What the fuck?"

"Yeah, man, he got fucked up on something and ran around town naked. Buncha kids saw him. Some nuns, too, I think."

"Are you screwing with me?"

Justin ignored the question and nodded at the living room section of the basement. A TV on a small credenza and a couch and bean bag. Movies and video games and empty beer cans littered the floor. "This is where we received our VHS education of terrible movies and stolen pornography."

"Probably the best days of our lives."

"Other things happened here, too."

"...Yeah."

"Two thousand. Fourteen years old." Justin patted the couch, stained with an assortment of liquids spilled over the years. "You, me, Shelly, Jessica."

"I couldn't believe they came over. I still can't."

"Shit, me neither. We were just a couple of punks. Hell, we were still eating our boogers at that point."

Ted cocked his head. "I...no, I wasn't."

Justin stopped and turned around. "What?"

"You ate snot when you were fourteen?"

"Uh. No. That...that was a joke." He laughed but it didn't seem too authentic. "The point is, we didn't deserve any kind of special service. We never did a thing for a couple of fine pieces of ass to be so kind. And yet...they came over. They spent the night. We were right there. You and Shelly on the floor, wrapped up in that retarded *Ren and Stimpy* blanket my mom made, and me and Jessica on the couch. Going at it like a goddamn orgy."

"You kept trying to talk to me during it."

"Jessica wasn't, uh, too happy about that."

"I think at one point you even tried to give me a high-five."

Justin shrugged like a high-five during sex was a perfectly normal thing to do. "I thought it was a moment worth celebrating."

"If I remember right, Jessica never talked to you after

that night."

"Wouldn't even return my calls."

"I wonder if the high-fiving thing was connected."

"I don't see how."

"Isn't she a nurse now?"

"Yeah, man. She works over at Franciscan. I ran into her once. She still fuckin' hates me."

"Just like the song."

Justin made a screwed-up face. "What?"

"That song."

"*What* song?"

"'She Fucking Hates Me'."

"That's what I just said."

"No, I'm saying—it's a song, too."

They stared at each other for a moment, not saying anything, then Justin shook his head. "*What?*"

Ted sighed. "Tell me again why we're talking about the night we lost our virginity?" The more they romanticized the past, the more he wanted to say screw all of this and return to Shelly's mom's. They'd been together since they were fourteen fucking years old. They couldn't *not* be together at this point. Why couldn't she see that?

Justin snorted out a laugh. "'Lost our virginity' sounds so girly."

"Well how else do you want me to say it?"

"I don't know. There has to be a more masculine phrasing. Like, uh…" He clicked his tongue against the roof of his mouth as he contemplated. "Like, hmm…debuted our jizz…or something."

"I will never, ever say that."

"Suit yourself." He giggled again. "*Lost our virginity…*"

"Well?"

"Well what?"

"Why are we talking about this?"

"Because, man. Don't you remember what we were watching?"

"What we were watching?"

"Yeah, on TV. My mom'd rented me the VHS before they went out to some party. Said to invite you over and have a movie night. Except halfway through the movie, we got naked and debuted our jizz."

"Please stop saying that."

"But after—after we finished—we rewound the movie and restarted it, since not a single one of us had been paying attention that first time."

"I can't imagine how a bunch of fourteen-years-olds could have been distracted."

"The movie, Teddy. Don't you remember?" He smiled and waited for Ted to answer.

"I have no idea."

Justin stiffened his posture and pointed at him. "I will not be threatened by a walking meat loaf!"

"Uh...what?"

He deflated a little. "A naked American man stole my balloons?"

"Justin. I really think we should go to the hospital."

"Come on. *An American Werewolf in London,* dude. Stop acting dumb."

"I haven't seen that movie in years."

"I think I've probably watched it ten times this week alone."

"That seems...excessive?"

"You asked what was wrong with me."

"You're addicted to horror movies?"

Justin started pacing in a circle and running his left hand through his hair while the other waved the revolver around. He moved with a limp that caused him to grimace slightly every time he used his leg. "Teddy, there's no good way to come out and say this."

"You're scaring me, man. Just tell me."

"You at least remember what the movie was about, right? I mean, hell, it's right there in the title."

"What movie?"

"The...the fucking *movie*. The one we're talking about."

"Okay, yeah, sure. The guy is hiking or some shit and gets bit by a werewolf, right?"

"Right..."

"I still don't understand."

"Teddy, think."

"I..."

"Teddy, goddammit." Justin stopped and stared at him. Defeated. Exhausted. "I'm a werewolf."

Ted wanted to laugh but couldn't find the courage. "Shut the fuck up."

"I'm serious."

"You're crazy."

"I might be crazy, yeah. I really might be crazy. But—" He stepped forward. "—But I might also be something else."

"Shit." Ted leaned against the concrete wall and wished he had a cigarette, despite not having had one in over seven years. "You're serious."

Justin held up the revolver. "There's silver bullets in this gun, Teddy. Real, legit silver bullets."

"What the fuck?"

"There's actually only two loaded. You wouldn't believe

how expensive these little bitches were."

"Where...where did you get silver bullets?"

"eBay, dude. Where else?"

"eBay." It sounded too ridiculous to be made-up.

"They have everything."

"Silver bullets. Because you're a werewolf."

"Well, that's the theory, yeah."

"I... I think I'm gonna go."

"Where you gotta go?"

"Shelly's expecting me. I told her I would be home by now."

Justin gave him a *cut-the-bullshit* look. "Come on, now. You and I both know that ain't true."

"What are you talking about?"

"I could sniff it on you the moment you walked through the door. Hell, just the sound of your voice from the way you answered the phone."

"I don't—"

"She left you, didn't she?"

Ted considered vomiting, then thought better of it. "No."

"You don't have to lie to me, man. I'm being pretty fuckin' truthful with you, wouldn't you say?"

"I would say you're being more psychotic than any-thing."

Justin paused, taking in that last comment and swigging it around. He gulped it down and looked back up at Ted. "How long has she been gone?"

"Look, I'm not talking about this right now. Not after all the shit you just laid on me."

"This is my last day on Earth. Tomorrow I won't be here for you to vent. Get it all off your chest, brother."

Ted shook his head. No way. "Why…why do you think you're a werewolf?"

Justin opened his mouth, then shut it. He turned and stared at the bathroom door then turned back to Ted, seeming to contemplate something. "Before I talk about that, answer me something."

"What?"

"Do you have to pee?"

"Do I have to…pee?"

"Yeah." Justin stared at him like he was an idiot.

Ted clicked his tongue. "Uh, no."

Justin pointed at the bathroom door. The lower half of the wood had been scratched to shit. "Well go try anyway."

"Why?"

"Trust me."

"I… I don't have to."

He paused, biting his lip, then threw up his hands in surrender. Ted flinched as the revolver jerked direction. "All right. Well, I do, so hold tight for a minute."

"What happened to the door? You get a dog or something?"

"All in due time, brother." He stopped just outside the bathroom and glanced over his shoulder. "Oh, and by the way, if you're gone when I'm done, I'll blow my brains out right here where I stand."

"Jesus Christ."

"Just making sure you and me's on the same page."

"Justin, man…"

"I'd rather wait until midnight, have you do the deed. But that don't mean I won't hesitate to do it myself if you pussy-out. Don't test me."

Justin entered the bathroom and left the door open.

The sound of urine splashing against water soon echoed through the basement.

Ted listened for a moment then decided fuck it and pulled out his cell phone. Still no texts, not from Shelly or anybody. He typed up a new message and clicked SEND: "I'm with Justin. He's going through some crazy shit. Need to talk to you. Please call. I love you."

Then he dialed 911 and hovered his thumb over the CALL button and debated pressing down.

The toilet flushed.

He cancelled the call and returned the phone to his pocket so it could continue its process of burning through his pants, burning through his flesh.

Justin sighed as he stepped out of the bathroom. "Oh man, you have no idea what a relief it is to see you still standing here. I'm in there, holding my pecker and thinking how much I really don't want to shoot myself."

"So you'll come to the hospital?"

"I didn't say I didn't want *you* to shoot me. I just mean, like, hell, can you imagine having to shoot *yourself*? That would take some strong motherfuckin' willpower, amigo."

"I don't want to shoot myself, Justin."

"Good. I wouldn't want you to, either. You're a good guy."

"I don't want to shoot you, either."

Justin grinned. "But you still came."

"Yeah, without knowing why you wanted me here."

"Don't you think it's a little bit of destiny that you *are* here, though? That you and I are here together?"

"Uh. Not really. You called. I came. That's what friends do."

"Friends also—"

Ted shook his head hard and fast. "Friends do not shoot

other friends in the face."

Justin tapped the revolver against his chest. "In the heart."

"*Or* in the heart."

"Shooting me in the head won't do a goddamn thing except piss me off. It's gotta be the heart. Okay? I'm being serious, dude."

"Friends don't shoot each other *anywhere*. Holy fucking shit."

"I believe your definition of friendship has been tainted in the years since we last saw each other."

"I think a lot of things have been tainted."

Justin laughed and scratched the side of his head with the tip of the revolver. "You really got no idea how true that statement is."

"So I'm beginning to gather."

"Follow me."

"Where are we going?"

He nodded to the doorless room at the end of the basement. It was by far the brightest area Ted had seen in the house today. "My bedroom."

"Why?"

"That's where it's going to happen."

"You're, uh, going to take a nap?"

"I reckon it'll be a bit more permanent than that."

SIX

WHEN THEY WERE KIDS, JUSTIN'S BEDROOM WALLS had been covered from floor to ceiling with magazine cut-outs of professional wrestling divas and random lingerie models he'd stumbled across in his mom's clothing catalogs. He kept a few spots reserved for the booklet covers of KoRn CDs. Back then, Jonathan Davis had been his god. Justin had this disgusting theory that the weird tongue-speaking in "Twist" represented how Davis sounded while performing cunnilingus. Ted had never successfully removed the imagery from his head.

Once upon a time the bedroom also had a kickass bunkbed and a footlocker full of comic books. Mostly DC but a few Marvels managed to slip in. Ted and Justin would sit on the floor for hours flipping through them, fantasizing how they'd react if inserted into similar situations. Underneath the comics, at the very bottom of the chest, Justin kept hidden a glorious collection of porno mags. They would wait until his parents were out of the house before finding the courage to dig them out. It didn't matter that Justin had the entire basement to himself. The fear of his mother sneaking in on them remained a constant danger throughout their childhood.

But now she was dead, and the porno mags were long gone. Same with everything else that'd once been in Justin's basement bedroom. Ted stood in it now and he didn't know how to react. It didn't feel like he was even in the same room.

The walls were covered in yellow nicotine stains and fist-sized holes. Against the wall opposite the unobstructed doorway, there was a deep freezer plugged in. Its dull hum wasn't immediately apparent. It seeped into Ted's senses and camouflaged itself into his thoughts as if it'd always been in his head, humming its song. A dirty, flat mattress had been left on the floor next to the right-side wall. A pile of chains and a large metal object Ted couldn't identify rested on the mattress, sinking its minimum cushioning against the cement floor.

"Holy shit. What did you do to this place?"

Justin shrugged. "Just a little rearranging."

"A little?" Ted stepped forward and inspected the metal thing on the mattress. "Jesus Christ, is that…is that an anchor?"

Justin grinned. Proud. "Sure is."

"Like from a ship?"

"Like from a ship."

Ted held his breath and focused on not freaking out. A gust of air exploded out of him and he pointed at the mattress like it was a dead body. "Why the fuck do you have an *anchor*? How did you even get one?"

"It was the heaviest object I could think of that would fit through my back door. And, well, I stole it. Duh."

"You stole it?"

"Yeah. From a ship."

"What ship?"

"I don't know, man. Some fuckin' fishing ship or whatever out on Lake Michigan. It was just left there on the shore. Like, nobody was in it or anything. How irresponsible, right?"

But Ted ignored him and crouched over the mattress, running his hand along the anchor's rusted metal. "Jesus, this thing's huge."

"Hey, I didn't invite you down here to talk about my dick, but I do appreciate the compliment all the same."

"How did you even get it down here?"

"Well, it wasn't easy. Truth be told, I'm guessing the lycan disease pumping through my veins has increased my strength quite a bit."

Ted looked over his shoulder, gripping the anchor for balance support. "The lycan disease."

"Teddy, I told you—"

"That you're a werewolf, yeah."

"Well, I wasn't joking."

Ted stood and wiped the rust stain that'd smeared across his hand against his pants. It didn't seem to want to come off, like maybe it was begging Ted to take it with him, get it far away from this house before it witnessed the homeowner do anything else crazy. "So you went and stole an anchor."

"That's right."

"But...why?"

"Because in case something goes wrong, you miss the shot, we need something to stop me from killing you."

"Something like an anchor."

"Correct."

"To stop you from killing me."

"When I transform, I will lose complete control. You

will no longer be my friend. Don't you understand? You'll just be this big juicy burger waitin' to be eaten up. I won't see you no different than my next meal."

Ted could have laughed if the sonofabitch didn't sound so sincere. "You're gonna eat me up?"

"Not if I can help it, brother. And not if you do your job and plug me where it counts."

"And that's your—"

"—my heart."

He pulled off his T-shirt and threw it behind him and tapped his chest with the barrel of the revolver. He'd drawn a giant bull's-eye there with a black Sharpie. Who knew how long ago. Not like he'd recently bathed or anything. Ted also noticed hundreds of scratch marks across his stomach, like Justin had been trying to rip off his flesh as if it were a suit he could take off and on at his leisure.

"Jesus Christ."

"I've taken care of everything. All you gotta do is not miss."

"What makes you think I won't? You act like I've fired a gun before. Like I'm some fuckin' champion gunslinger or something."

"You always kicked my ass in *GoldenEye*."

"This is a real gun, Justin. Not some Nintendo 64 controller."

"It's not that hard. You can do it." He winked. "I got faith in ya, brother."

It was a challenge not to point at him and scream that he was crazy over and over until he lost his voice. "Maybe, maybe not. But the thing is, I'm not—I'm not doing this. This is crazy. There's a ship anchor in your room and you've drawn a target on your chest and you have a gun with silver bullets and none of this is making any goddamn sense."

"You think I don't realize that? Hell, man, how do you think I feel? I've been dealing with this shit by myself for months now. I've about lost my fuckin' mind."

"Then let—"

"If you say let you take me to a hospital one more time, I'm going to put both of these goddamn bullets to good use."

"Now you're threatening me. Awesome."

Justin grabbed his own hair with his free hand and yanked it upward, grunting. "Well, you're refusing to fucking listen."

"When you start making sense, maybe I'll start listening."

"Goddammit, Teddy. Don't you get it? We're running out of time here." He held up his hand as if he had a watch strapped to his wrist, then realized it was bare and slumped his shoulders. "We gotta start picking up the pace."

"Uh...picking up the pace *how*?"

"Okay, first, what I'm about to do—don't freak out."

"I'm already freaking out." He crossed his arms over his chest and tapped his foot against the cement and watched.

"Seriously. Don't run away or try to call anybody. I'm doing this to protect you."

Justin laid the revolver on the mattress and picked up the chains next to it. The chains were connected to the anchor. He wrapped them around his body, between his legs, and around his neck.

"You're really doing this."

"I told you. It's for your own good. If you're not quick enough to take the shot, I'll fucking rip you in half. I won't be able to stop myself."

"Justin, werewolves aren't real."

He secured the padlock and let it drop. "Says the guy who ain't one."

SEVEN

J USTIN HELD OUT THE KEY AND REVOLVER AND TED stared at them without blinking. "What are you doing?"

"You gotta take this stuff."

"But I don't want it."

"Look. Just take it, okay? Come midnight, if I'm still normal, if you're right and I'm just some crazy person, then you can unlock the chains and drive me wherever the hell you please. But if I start to turn—like I know I'm gonna—then there's nobody else I can count on to save me. You gotta blow me away, buddy. You gotta shoot me right in the fucking heart."

"I always thought you had to shoot a werewolf in the head. Destroy the brains." Ted aimed a finger gun at Justin's head and pulled the trigger.

Justin flinched.

"Nah, man, that's...that's zombies." He sighed and waved the items at him. "Will you take this more seriously, please? This is my life we're talking about here."

"Okay, fine, fuck."

Teddy stuffed the key in his pants pocket and held the gun out, staring at it like it was some kind of alien artifact.

"I can't believe someone sold you this."

"Shit, dude, I could've bought a fuckin' grenade if I wanted to. People will sell you anything if you have the money."

"And since when do you have money?"

"When my parents died, I collected on their life insurance. Haven't had to get a job in years."

"Must be nice."

"For a little while, sure. But look how I ended up." He gestured both thumbs inward. "I'm chained to a fucking ship anchor."

"You chained yourself, though."

"Yeah, and for good reason."

Ted couldn't keep looking at him chained up like that. The situation couldn't have been more ridiculous.

The gun was heavy in his hand. It was the first time he'd ever held a firearm and he hated it. In movies whenever someone picks up a gun for the first time in their lives, they act like it's the greatest thing in the world. They claim they feel invincible, that it's like having a second cock. Ted was convinced whoever wrote those movies had never actually touched a gun before, because there wasn't anything macho about this at all. He didn't feel like the king of any damn thing. He was holding a death machine and nobody had ever properly trained him how to handle it. It seemed like all it'd take would be one wrong jerk of his hand and he'd accidentally blow a hole in someone. Also, the idea of having two cocks freaked him out. What would he do with an extra one? Would he have to buy pants with two zippers? The whole concept was simply illogical. One cock was just fine, in his book.

He set the revolver on the deep freezer. Justin couldn't make him keep holding it, not for anything.

The deep freezer had a padlock hanging from its latch and Ted wondered why a man who lived alone had to lock up his food. He caressed the steel of the lock, smooth and barely used.

Justin smacked his face with his open palm and the sound echoed. He winced and squeezed his fist and rubbed his knuckles against his teeth like maybe he'd hit himself harder than intended. "Ah, shit, I just realized I forgot to bring the beer down."

"Take the key back then. I don't even want this shit." Ted started to reach into his pocket but Justin waved him off.

"Nah, man. You can go get it, can't you? It's just upstairs, in the fridge."

"I don't know."

Justin scrunched his brow. "What do you mean, you don't know? I'm a werewolf chained to a ship anchor. You can go get the beer. Come on."

"Can werewolves even drink beer?"

"This one sure as fuck does."

"Okay. Fine. Shit."

"Don't bring them all, though. Warm beer is the grossest thing in the world. Start me off with two. And whatever you want."

Ted patted the deep freezer. "Why can't we just put them in there?"

Justin hesitated and scratched the back of his neck. "It's locked."

"Don't you have a key?"

He shook his head. "Lost it a while back."

"What's in it?"

"What?"

"What's so special you had to put a lock on it in the first place?"

"Oh. I was trying to preserve my meat rations. Kept overdoing it. Those last couple days before a full moon hits? They're a killer, bro."

Ted studied the deep freezer with wonder. "So there's a bunch of meat in there?"

"Yeah."

"And you lost the key."

"Guilty as charged."

Ted hunched over, squinting at the padlock. "I'm pretty sure I could pick this."

"Nah, that's okay."

"It doesn't even look that strong. Could probably just hit it with a hammer, bust it open."

"I'll take that advice under consideration."

"You were just pissed off that I didn't bring enough McDonald's, and this whole time you got a deep freezer of extra meat."

"Yeah, but it's not thawed. Who's got the patience for frozen meat?" Justin spat out something that looked like a tiny organ. It splattered against the wall. "Now, for the love of god—will you please go get me a fuckin' beer?"

Ted considered further questioning but realized he didn't care enough to bother. He walked upstairs and grabbed a Pabst Blue Ribbon from the fridge. He sat at the kitchen table and checked his phone for updates, careful not to step in the puddle of spilled McDonald's. He started typing out a new message to Shelly, then deleted it. If she hadn't answered the dozens of texts he'd already sent her, one more wasn't going to make any difference. At this point her silence was enough of a response.

He popped open the beer and scrolled his social media feed while he drank. He didn't look at Facebook too often. That was more Shelly's thing. It wasn't that he didn't understand how to use it, it was more that he just didn't see the point. If he wanted to be social, he'd just go out to the bar or invite a buddy over to watch a game with him. It perplexed him, the idea that people needed to be social twenty-four-seven. When he thought about it, he was happiest when he didn't have to talk to anyone or put on a show of manners. When it was just him and Shelly kicking back on the couch with a few cold ones and something loud and dumb on the TV.

But a lot of people liked doing the social media thing, including Shelly. Except Shelly hadn't been online since yesterday, so either she'd tampered with her settings so he couldn't see the little green circle next to her name, or she actually hadn't logged on. The former seemed plausible. She'd blocked him a few times in the past during other fights. But the latter? He couldn't conceive of a reality where Shelly didn't post at least one rant on her feed a day. She liked to refer to Facebook as free therapy. You log on and rant and drain all the stress you've been building up throughout the day and suddenly you feel like a new person. She'd laid out this whole presentation to him one night after they got home from the bar. He'd made fun of her for spending more time looking at the screen than real life. She spoke for nearly an hour before he managed to convince her that he finally understood the great social media mystery and got her to undress and straddle him on the couch.

When he tried to think about it now, he couldn't even remember the last time they'd had sex. The last time they'd looked at each other with true affection. Held each other's hand or smiled in their peripheries. Offered a compliment without company nearby to overhear. The last time they'd actually tried to make things work.

Fuck it.

He finished off the beer and tossed it across the kitchen. The empty can landed in the sink and joined its disemboweled cousins. The fridge was loaded with beer. All of it Pabst Blue Ribbon, the same shit they'd been guzzling since middle school. He grabbed four more cans and returned to the basement.

Sweat poured down Justin's bare chest as he pulled at the chains retraining him. At the sight of Ted, he stopped struggling and collapsed on the mattress, half-crying, half-laughing.

"Oh my god, I thought you'd left me. I thought you'd actually left."

Ted held out two of the PBRs and Justin grabbed them and popped one of the tabs open and started guzzling it down his throat before Ted could respond.

"I was just taking a breather. I don't know how we were ever able to stand sleeping down here. The humidity is malevolent."

Justin shrugged, then belched and squashed the now-empty can of PBR and pegged it at the wall behind Ted. "I've slept in this basement every night since I was seven years old. It ain't no thang, brother. It ain't no thang."

Ted grimaced, thumb paused under the tab of his own beer. "Don't say 'thang'."

"Fuck you. 'Thang' is cool as hell. Besides, you ain't allowed to tell me how to talk if you're gonna say nerdy-ass shit like *malevolent*. And if you're hot, follow the lead of your buddy Justin here and take off your shirt. You'll be amazed at the difference."

"I'm not taking off my shirt."

"Why? You get a weird nipple piercing or something?"

Ted thought about it for a moment, sipping his PBR. "Me standing here with a gun while you're sitting there chained with no shirt on is crazy enough. But if we both were shirtless, I don't know, somehow it makes it twice as strange."

Justin nodded and swigged beer from cheek to cheek. "You know. I suspect what you just said right then might've been homophobic, but I'm not one-hundred-percent certain."

"You might be right."

"You fucking homophobic piece of shit." He laughed and leaned back against the wall, resting his shoulder against the ship anchor like it was an old friend.

"Justin, what are we doing? Are we seriously going to just hang out here all night?"

"That's the plan."

"It's a pretty dumb plan."

"I don't see you with a better one."

"Well, for starters, I still operate in a reality that does not include the existence of…" Ted interrupted himself with a gulp of beer, too afraid to finish his sentence. No, not afraid. Embarrassed.

"Go on, say it."

He swallowed and wiped his mouth. "Werewolves."

"I swear, the more you say the word, the less ridiculous it starts to sound."

"Uh-huh."

"Do you think I happily accepted this fate? One day I

just woke up and decided I'm gonna be a fuckin' were-wolf?"

"I don't know what I think."

"Sure you do. Right now, you're thinking about calling the police. What's stopping you? You have the gun, after all. Plus I'm chained up. I ain't goin' nowhere, right?"

Ted nodded. Sure. "It's crossed my mind."

"More than once, I reckon."

"You have to admit you'd feel obligated to do the same, put in my shoes."

"I refuse to admit shit, because I ain't in your shoes, now am I? That's not what's happening. The truth of the situation is, you're the one with the gun and I'm the one chained up and claiming to be some goddamn supernatural beast. The cards ain't exactly in my favor here."

Ted pulled his cell phone out of his pocket and held it up like it was a Bible. "Then why don't I call?"

"Because you're my friend, and I am begging you to give me a chance. I gave you the gun on my own free will and I am telling you, nothing good will come with me out of captivity."

"I can't stay here all night, Justin." Ted's vision left Justin and trained itself on the phone screen, staring at the unanswered texts he'd sent Shelly. They weren't even marked as READ. "I have to get home. I have a wife."

"But she isn't waiting for you."

Ted looked up. Anger sizzling. "You don't know that."

"You've been checking your phone like every two minutes. If she hasn't responded to your texts yet, she ain't gonna."

"She will."

"What did you do?"

"What makes you think I did anything?"

"Because you're the one waiting for her to text back, not the other way around."

"I...I don't want to talk about that."

"You should. It'll help."

"Help what?"

Justin shrugged and opened his second PBR. "Help you relax, help you come to terms with life."

"*Come to terms with life?* Right now I'm standing in your basement holding a fucking gun. You're—"

"Well, you ain't exactly holding it, if you want to get technical about the whole thing." He nodded at the deep freezer.

Ted sighed. "Okay, so I'm standing in your basement *next* to a gun. You're chained to an anchor with a target drawn on your chest. I'm—"

"—Man, you got no clue how long it took me to do that. Even standing in front of a mirror, shit was tricky as sin."

"—I'm not coming to terms with life for a very long time."

Justin paused, letting the words sink in as he sipped his beer. He tapped the back of his skull against the wall and spit something red and thick on the floor next to the mattress. "Maybe after this is all finished, after I'm out of the picture for good. Maybe then."

"Yeah, maybe."

"Teddy, look—I'm sorry things aren't working out too well with you and Shelly."

"It's fine. It'll pass. We're just having a rough spell. It won't last."

"You'll be okay, brother."

"And what about you?"

"Ask me again come midnight."

"Can werewolves talk?"

"Hell if I know."

"I thought—"

"Yeah, but I ain't got no recollection of what I'm like when transformed into my wolf-form. It's like I'm blackout drunk. One minute I'm here, then I'm waking up the next morning, naked and covered in blood that don't belong to me."

"You woke up covered in blood?"

Justin hesitated, then slowly nodded. "A few times, yeah."

"What the fuck." Ted gripped his beer can with both hands to prevent dropping it.

"Usually somewhere in the woods. Once I was in a pond. Maybe it was a puddle. Either way, I nearly drowned."

"Justin—"

"Why don't you sit down?"

"I don't want to sit down."

"Standing like that is just gonna make you more stressed."

Ted sighed and sat on top of the deep freezer, the gun next to his thigh. "I'm still stressed."

"Yeah, no shit."

"Justin, tell me what happened."

He nodded at the wall, where the bathroom would be in the other room. "You sure you don't gotta piss first? I swear I can hear the pee begging to explode from your bladder. Like it's speaking directly at me. Screaming for help."

"…What?"

"Are. You. Sure."

"I'm…I'm positive." Although, now that Ted thought about it, he kind of *did* have to urinate, but he wasn't about to admit it now after Justin started talking like a crazy person.

"Because this isn't gonna be short. Just fair warning."

"Well, the way you talk, we have to kill time until midnight, anyway."

"Right you are, brother. Right you are." He finished off his beer and belched and more of the crimson glop shot out of his mouth. "Okay. So. What I'm about to tell you, you're not gonna like. I'm not too proud of my actions, and I know you're going to judge me like some kinda goddamn Christian, but this is who I am, and there ain't no changing that."

"I'm not going to judge you."

"We'll see about that.

"What is it, man?"

Justin stared at his empty beer can for a full minute before he answered, and when he finally did, he refused to look Ted in his eyes. "Dogfighting, okay? I—I got into dogfighting."

EIGHT

"**D**OGFIGHTING?"

"Yeah."

"Jesus fuck."

"Maybe you oughta go fetch us a couple more beers before we continue. We—we're gonna need 'em."

Justin buried his face in his palms and groaned, like he was being grilled by a ruthless detective in an intense interrogation. And in a way, maybe he was.

Ted didn't bother arguing this time. He hopped off the deep freezer and progressed halfway across the room before he paused and glanced over his shoulder at the revolver. He wondered if maybe it'd be a good idea to take it with him. But then he wondered why he'd even wonder such a thing. Justin was scrambling his goddamn brain, he swore to God.

He stumbled upstairs and retrieved an untampered six-pack of PBR. On the way back down, he made a detour into the bathroom and pissed out the last couple beers he'd mainlined. He flushed and pushed the door open with his foot and returned to Justin's room. He was still sitting on the mattress against the anchor, grinning like a fool.

"I knew you had to pee."

"You didn't know anything."

He pointed to his temple and leaned forward. "Were-wolf senses, dawg."

"You do not have werewolf senses."

"You got no idea what I have, man."

Ted tore off a PBR from the ring and pegged it at Justin. It struck him in the crotch and he doubled over on the mattress, cursing and grunting.

"Dude, what the fuck was that?"

"I thought you had werewolf senses."

Justin coughed and picked up the PBR and flipped him off. "You're such an asshole."

"Speaking of assholes." Ted popped the tab on a new beer. Foam spurted out and splashed on him. "You mentioned something about dogfighting."

Justin held up a wait-a-minute finger and gulped down his own PBR. Afterward he sat for a moment not saying anything, like he was choosing his words wisely, which would have been a first for him. "You remember No-Dick Rick, right?"

"How could I not?"

"He was one of a kind, wasn't he?"

"He was something, all right."

"Okay, so, like a year ago, not even, I call him up trying to score some weed. My usual guy, he decided to retire, said he needed to be responsible now or some shit since he was gonna be a dad. Something lame like that."

"How dare he."

"Right?" Justin shook his head, disgusted. "Real fuckin' scumbag move."

"Definitely."

"So you're craving a joint and your usual guy's out of

the game. What do you do, right? You start probing back to all the people who ever dealt to you throughout the years. High school fuckboys. Barfly hotheads. Burger King drive-thru cashiers. And you gotta think to yourself: who else do you call during such emergencies? Out of all of 'em, who do you think's gonna still be the most reliable? Why, No-Dick Rick, of course."

Ted cocked his head, smelling a slightly different odor when it came to their teen years. "I don't think anybody's ever considered that guy reliable once in his life."

"Oh come on. You know what I mean. He was the man back in high school, figured he'd still be the man now. And you know what? I wasn't let down. Dude practically has his own ganja jungle growing at his house." He rested his beer between his thighs and connected each hand by his fingertips, then made an explosion sound with his mouth and slowly separated his hands, maybe demonstrating the expansive nature of No-Dick Rick's setup, maybe having a stroke. Ted wasn't sure.

Ted cleared his throat and ignored the weird hand motions. "You've been there? To, uh, Rick's house?"

Justin leaned his head back against the wall and smiled. Remembering a better time, a better life. "Yeah, man. It's paradise."

Ted tried to imagine it. "I haven't smoked in years."

"Do you miss it?"

"Shelly doesn't like it."

"Yeah, but, *do you miss it?*"

"Hell yeah, I miss it. Of course I miss it."

"You know, I got a little around here probably. I'd say we kick back and smoke up one last time, but I'm afraid you'll need to be at your best tonight. Need you alert, ready to go. I can't have you getting stoned and accidentally wasting one of the silver bullets on my arm or something. Those motherfuckers are expensive."

"Right. We wouldn't want that."

"If you're shooting me, I want it to be over as quickly as possible. Pegging me in the arm ain't gonna accomplish shit."

"If you're so concerned about my aim, maybe we oughta quit drinking."

Justin laughed and held up his can. "PBR hardly qualifies as drinking."

Ted thought about it and nodded. He had a point.

Justin adjusted his sitting position and continued the story. "So, anyway, I call up good ol' No-Dick Rick, tell him what I want and all that, and he says sure, says he's in the area anyway, that he'll stop by my house after he's finished with some errands."

"*Your* house?"

"Who do you think my parents left it to—the goddamn pope? Of course it's my house."

"Okay, okay, calm down. Shit."

"Don't think I don't know what people say about me, man."

"I don't know what you're talking about."

"They say I got it made, that I'm this spoiled little kid who's never gonna grow up, never gonna leave his parents' basement."

"Nobody says that."

"And you know what? They're right. But tonight—this is my last night here, and I'll be leaving one of two ways: in a body bag or a straitjacket."

"I vote the straitjacket."

"Well, yeah, me too. But if I...transform, we're not gonna have a lot of say in the matter. Ain't no straitjacket in the world gonna imprison a werewolf."

"Just ship anchors."

Justin patted the anchor like it was his son. "We can hope, at least."

"How did No-Dick Rick...uh, lose his dick, anyway?"

"What? I don't fucking know. That's not exactly something you can ask somebody. Jesus Christ. Where are your manners?"

"True."

"However—if you really want to know the truth—I did consider asking him about it, that day he stopped by the house. Hell, the question's bound to be on the tip of everybody's tongue, right? Just nobody's got the balls—"

"Especially Rick."

"Wh-what?"

Ted paused, unsure his joke had landed. "You know. Like his name. No-Di—"

"Nobody's ever said anything about the man's balls. For Christ's sake. Show No-Dick some respect."

"I just assumed—"

"*Anyway.* Like I said. I was actually considering asking how he got the name, but I was too worried about pissing him off, and he'd just leave without hooking me up, so I kept my mouth shut. Which, of course, is always the wise move when dealing with a man nicknamed 'No-Dick'. So, he brings in this fuckin' huge pit bull and we chill out on the couch, watching TV, I forget what, some dumb daytime shit. Then I try to blow smoke in his dog's face, get that contact high going—you know, how we used to do with Bobby's cat?—and Rick, he just flips the fuck out, says that isn't no dog you can get high, that there is what he called a professional. 'A professional what?' I asked, and he goes, 'A professional fighter, motherfucker, what you think?'"

"I'm surprised the dog didn't bite your face off."

"Shit, me too." Justin touched his face, making sure it was still there. "But I ain't ever made the best decisions while high. Or sober, come to think about it."

"It's a stigma we all gotta deal with—us Hammond kids. None of us are too smart."

"At least you were smart enough to get out."

"But apparently not smart enough to stay that way."

"You know, Teddy, after tonight I don't see why you'll ever have a reason to return."

"I do what you want me to do, and I'm gonna end up serving a life sentence in some cell."

"Not if you listen, pay attention, and do exactly what I say. I've already planned everything out. Trust me, you'll be fine."

"And you?"

"Well, Teddy, I'll be dead."

Both their eyes fell upon the revolver on the deep freezer.

Ted bit his lip. "That's the part I don't like."

"Shit, you think I like it? It is what it is, brother. I've come to accept it and soon you will, too."

"I don't see how."

"Then let me tell my fucking story."

NINE

"So Rick, he tells me his dog's a professional fighter, and I'm like, 'whoa, okay, that's kinda weird.' Kinda cruel, I guess was my first impression. And I told him that, yeah, right to his face, kinda blurted it out, to be honest, wasn't intentional, and he goes, 'Nah, dude, these dogs, they're born to fight, it's in their blood, it's what they love to do most. Just like humans, they're alive to die.'"

Ted raised his brow, swishing the last couple drops of beer around in the can. "He said humans are alive to die?"

"Are you calling me a liar?"

"I don't know. It just sounds fake. Like something from *True Detective.*"

"I never bothered with that HBO bullshit."

Ted shrugged. "Some of it's pretty good. Shelly was the one who wanted us to get it. She's in love with that *Game of Thrones* show."

"People don't shut the fuck up about that one."

"It's all right."

Justin seemed to contemplate it. "Well, come midnight, if it turns out I'm just nuts, I'll give it a chance once I'm out of the loony bin."

"You really gonna let me take you?"

"Shit. You think I honestly want to get shot?"

Ted pointed a new can of PBR at the target drawn on Justin's chest. "I'm just saying. You've come prepared, is all."

Justin opened his mouth to speak but fell into another coughing fit. He wiped his mouth and the back of his hand got smeared with blood. He spat over the side of the mattress and cleared his throat and sipped his beer. "But like I was saying. No-Dick Rick says weird shit all the time. You know that. Hell, another thing he told me—this was after he convinced me to come with him to his next fight—we're driving to the place—you know, where the fight's gonna happen—and he points out the window and says some shit like… 'Justin, one day this entire town will be in flames, and the last thing we'll hear is the laughter of God as he blows us out.'"

"What the fuck does that mean?"

"Shit, you think I know? I'm just in the back seat, staring at a pit bull and hoping like hell it don't attack me, and now this dude's saying all types of crazy shit. I'm just happy to get out of the car with all my fingers intact. We pull up at this abandoned K-Mart—you remember those, right?"

"Sure. Haven't seen one in a long time."

"Yeah, neither had I. And this one—shit, it hadn't been opened in years. Barely remembered going there when I was a kid, getting those British Knights I loved for some fuckin' reason. Goddamn, probably the lamest shoes on Earth right there."

"They were right up there." Ted glanced at Justin's feet now. Bare save for the layer of dirt encompassing them. Like his fingers, he'd gone far too long since the last time he cut his toenails. Little jagged razor blades attached to the tip of each toe. Ted grimaced and quickly looked away.

"So we drive around the K–Mart, toward the back, and get out and Rick does this special knock against one of the giant metal doors. You know, those big-ass garage doors you'd pull into to get your car looked at or whatever."

"I don't remember K-Mart having an automotive section."

"Well, maybe this was used for delivery trucks. What are you, the goddamn K-Mart police now? What the fuck does it matter?"

"I guess it doesn't."

"The knock, it wasn't that complex. I mean, this is No-Dick Rick we're talking about here. If he could memorize it, then it's a good sign the club wasn't that much of a secret. It was like...ba-da-ba, ba-da-ba, ba-da, ba-da, da, da, some shit like that."

"I think that's the same knock the CIA uses."

"El-oh-el if you think the CIA bothers to knock."

Ted cocked his head. "Did you just say 'el-oh-el'?"

"The occasion called for it."

"You really have changed."

"Don't you fucking know it. Anyway, he knocks, maybe a minute passes, I start thinking I'm being set-up, that no-body's here, and this fuckin' guy is just gonna sic his dog on my ass and rob me blind, but then some dude's head pops up through the little window there, looks us both over, nods, then pulls open the door. We gotta bend over to get inside, like the door gets jammed halfway up, but it's no big deal, whatever, I can limbo when I gotta."

"Can werewolves limbo?"

"Fuck you, man. You'll find out, don't you worry about that."

"Uh-huh."

"All right, so, this place is a real shit-hole, right? We

limbo ourselves in and it's mostly just this big empty room, some torn-up couches and folding chairs spread here and there, but in the middle of the room, there's these stacks of bricks outlined in a huge circle, and it's obvious that's where the magic happens."

"Dogfighting is magic?"

"It's an expression."

"A terrible expression."

"Whatever. If you trained dogs to fight, you'd consider that circle magic. The expression works. Shut up. So, okay, all the people inside this place, first off, they're all guys, not a chick in sight, which I guess isn't a surprise considerin' dogfighting ain't the most feminine of activities."

"I'm pretty sure that's sexist."

"So complain about it on your blog."

"I stopped updating my blog years ago."

"After tonight, you may wanna reconsider."

"Sure. Everybody will be dying to hear about my insane friend who thought he was a werewolf."

"You might even land a movie deal."

"You think they'll get a real ship anchor for the set?"

"Shit, I'll be dead anyway, they can just use this one."

"You don't think it'll be locked up in evidence?"

"Good point. They may need to invest in another. I'm sure they'll have enough in their budget for a ship anchor."

"If they don't, I'll boycott the movie."

"You're a true friend. But back to this K-Mart sausage fest. These were some sketchy motherfuckers, dude. I mean, yeah, this is Hammond, everybody looks sketchy, but these guys were like escaped-convict-sketchy. I immediately started telling myself not to open my mouth, 'cause you know more than anybody, once I start talking, I ain't gonna shut up, and the odds of me saying some stupid shit that'll piss somebody off are pretty high."

"It's extremely probable, yes."

"So I kinda hang back behind Rick and his scary-ass pit bull. Rick walks up to this one dude, this ghetto accountant guy, and they talk about the latest episode of *The Walking Dead* for a few, then—"

"They talked about *The Walking Dead?*"

"Yeah, that's what I said. So what? It's a popular show."

"I'm just having a hard time imagining these two guys talk about a zombie show while dogs fight each other to death a few feet away."

"Well, the dogs weren't fighting yet. All the bets were still being made, I guess. Rick, he asks me how much I'm gonna put down for his dog to win, and I'm like, dude, I barely had enough cash on me for the weed, I can't afford to start gambling on no dogfights. He kind of gets upset then, says something like he brought me all the way down here and I'm not even grateful enough to support him. Which, I mean, that's weird, right? Rick and I aren't even really friends. I just wanted to get high, and now he's trying to get me to place bets for him. Maybe he was lonely, I don't know. I got to feeling bad for him, so I put down a hundred."

"You gambled a hundred dollars on dogfighting?"

"Don't you fucking judge me, dude. You weren't there. It was super awkward, all those tough guys staring at me as Rick moped around because I wasn't offering any support. I'm telling you, losing your dick really turns you into a little bitch."

"I can't imagine it would be a pleasant experience."

"The only pleasant experience with dogfighting is

when you win, and that's exactly what I did. Doubled my money right there on the spot. Rick's dog was a vicious motherfucker, dude, you have no idea. As soon as the fight started, the other dog didn't stand a chance, it was done for, fuckin' *lunchmeat*."

"Did it die?"

"Nah. The owner called the fight before Rick's dog could finish him off, and let me tell you, that dog *really* wanted to finish him. He had that death-gaze going. Scary shit. But…I don't know. Kind of exciting, too."

Justin looked up at him, hopeful, but Ted shot him down. "This is really fucked up."

"I'm not arguing that, because yeah, man, it totally *is* fucked up, no doubt about it. But in the heat of the moment, when it's just you and a bunch of other dudes standing in a circle, shouting and cheering these two crazy beasts to fight like glorious gladiators? It's something else altogether. But I don't expect you to understand, so it's all right. I didn't get it until I was there in the circle with the rest of 'em. And even then, it didn't immediately click. But once that rush hit me, oh holy fuck did it hit."

Justin wrapped his arms around his shins and rested his jaw on his knees and rocked back and forth. Excited. Nervous.

"I started going back every Saturday night, for about…I don't know, three months maybe? Sometimes I lost, sure, but not too often. It was like I'd found my calling or some shit, bettin' on the dogs, knowing which one had the right stuff, the killing genes."

"You went more than once?"

"You win a jackpot on a slot, there's a good chance you ain't gonna cash in and go home, never gamble again. Of course I went back. This shit, it's more addicting than any shit we ever put in our bodies. This is the real deal, man, these pups."

"I think I'm going to throw up."

"You know where the bathroom is."

"Ugh. There's a point to this story, right?"

"Well, I'm getting there, ain't I?"

"I…don't know."

"Pop me off another, would you." Justin reached out and opened and closed his hand over and over until Ted tossed a PBR into it. He pressed the side of the can against his face and closed his eyes, breathing heavy. "Okay, now, this next part is gonna make you wanna say a whole bunch of ugly things at me, and you would be completely in the right to say such ugly things, but please just hold off until I'm done, all right? This ain't exactly the easiest of confessions."

"Okay."

"Thank you. Now, well, okay, so at this point I'm going down to the K-Mart every Saturday, placing my bets on other people's dogs, right? Well, it gets to where I'm starting to get bored, like something's missing, and for a while I can't quite place what. But then it hits me: to fully immerse myself in this scene, I'm gonna need to get my own dog, my own fighter. I need to become a trainer."

"Oh Jesus Christ."

"Remember what I said—"

"Oh, fuck what you said." Justin stood up off the deep freezer and paced in front of the mattress setup, lifting the can of beer up to his lips and lowering it without drinking. A robot fulfilling its destiny. "Are you serious? *You got a dog?*"

"Well. Kind of." He licked the foam off the top of the beer can.

"Kind of?"

"Let me finish the story."

"Go ahead. Finish the story about your wacky adventures in dogfighting. Holy fucking shit. You got a fucking dog. Are you goddamn serious?"

Justin waited. "Are you done?"

Ted thought about it. He could have easily continued. He waved him on. "Just get it over with."

"Thank you. Now, of course I don't know where to get a proper fightin' dog, so I call up No-Dick and ask him for some help, and he tells me that you don't find the dog, the dog finds you, which...come on, that's bullshit, but whatever. I ask him where his dog found him at then, and he says the pound, and I tell him it sounds a whole lot like he was the one who found the dog after all, and he gets all angry and offended and tells me to go fuck myself, which is pretty ironic coming from a guy with no dick, but whatever. I end up just going to the pound, but none of the dogs they got there are anywhere close to what anybody would ever consider tough. I'm talkin', like, bulldogs and chihuahuas and shit."

"Aww."

"Yeah, adorable, sure, but fighters? Nah, man. They'd get their throats ripped out in a goddamn second."

"But it's okay when they're pit bulls?"

"At least they can put up a fight."

"You're going to Hell, I hope you realize that."

"Well, that's the plan, anyway."

TEN

THE BEER WAS STARTING TO HIT TED, SO HE SAT DOWN on the cement with his back against the deep freezer and popped the tab on a fresh one. He saw no reason in stopping now. At this point, he was all in.

Justin motioned for another as well and Ted rolled one across the room. He scooped it up and opened it and held it between his legs without bothering to take a drink. The foam rushed over his sweatpants. He didn't seem to mind. "So, after I struck out at the pound, I tried calling No-Dick again, but of course he didn't answer. That guy is the most sensitive drug dealer on the planet, I swear to Christ. But I'm resourceful, I can get things done by myself. I went on Craigslist, and what do you know? Place is a goldmine of pits looking for homes."

"Homes, or fighting arenas?"

"Teddy. Come on."

"Oh, that's right. They're the same thing. I forgot."

"Real mature, judging a man on the night of his death."

"Well, if I judge you tomorrow, how will you know?"

Justin sighed. "Craigslist."

"Right."

"It was like I was a kid strollin' through a toy store. And

you know, they weren't as expensive as you'd expect. Most ran for about two, two-fifty. Shit, I'd made that much on that first fight with Rick, so you can imagine how much cash I was drowning in three months later." He held up his hand and curled his fingers into a C, like he was holding a thick stack of cash.

"And you can't even swim."

"I can too swim."

"You sink faster than that stupid anchor you're chained to."

"Don't knock the anchor. This thing is going to end up saving your life, just you wait and see."

"That and these silver bullets." Ted reached up over his head and blindly felt around for the revolver on top of the deep freezer. His fingers curled around the handle and he brought it down in his lap. It looked so stupid and ridiculous. It was hard to believe it possessed the power to kill a man.

"You laugh about 'em now, but soon enough them silver bullets are gonna be the only things preventing me from tearing you limb from limb."

"Because silver bullets kill werewolves."

"You bet your ass."

"Shouldn't I be betting on this new dog of yours?"

Deep breath. "Maybe not."

Ted pointed the revolver at the wall and mouthed the word *bang*. "The dog thing didn't work out?"

"Do you see a dog around here?"

"I don't know, it could be—"

"There ain't no dog, man. Never was."

He set the revolver down on the ground next to him and offered Justin his full attention. "You came to your senses and realized dogfighting is evil?"

"Well, not exactly."

"Uh-huh."

"What happened was, I found this one entry that seemed too good to be true."

"Oh, one of those."

"Yeah, one of those."

"I'm gonna go ahead and assume it *was* too good to be true."

"You're skipping ahead in the story, but yeah, you might be on to somethin' there."

"Oh man. Maybe I have werewolf senses, too."

"You're such a dick." Justin hid his mouth behind his fist as he laughed. "Anyway, this guy, the one I found on Craigslist, he has this post claiming he's got a dog specifically raised to kill. The *meanest* of the *meanest*. The *deadliest* of the *deadliest*. Says when this dog was a pup, he sucked the tit of a coyote infected with rabies."

"Haha, what? That—that doesn't sound like a thing."

"Well that's what it said. Also, there was this note toward the end of the ad, about how the dog had already killed itself a man."

"It said the dog killed somebody?"

"I guess there was this burglar, he broke through the window, and the dog freaked out, tore the dude's throat out of his neck like it was nothing."

"Jesus."

"Yeah."

"That's one fucked-up advertisement."

"A smart one, too, considerin' that's exactly the kinda dog I was after."

"A dog that kills humans?"

"A monster."

"If I'm learning anything from this story, it's that Craigslist needs to go over their policy and rethink what they allow to be listed."

"Ain't against the law to sell a dog."

"Yeah, but, I don't know, it seems like there's probably some kind of code of conduct broken when you advertise that the dog's killed somebody before."

"Are you a lawyer?"

"What?"

"Are. You. A. Lawyer?"

"Fuck off."

"Yeah. Neither am I."

Ted offered him a raised middle finger and Justin accepted it with grace. "So I called the number listed with the ad and it doesn't even ring, right? Goes straight to voicemail. Some robot chick saying the usual, thank you for calling, leave a message and they'll return my call as soon as possible. And I do, I leave a message, just a quick, 'hey, I might want to buy the dog you advertised on Craigslist', and I go take a piss and before I can even finish, my phone's ringing. I race back in the kitchen, dick still hanging out, little trickles of pee getting all over my goddamn pants, all over the floor. I answer it and this dude, he asks if I'm still interested in the dog, the one on Craigslist—except he doesn't call it a dog, no, he calls it *the animal*—and I tell him no shit I'm still interested, it hasn't even been but two minutes since I called, and...and get this, okay? He asks me if I'm a *vegetarian*."

Ted waited for a punchline but Justin just stared at him. "Why...why would that matter?"

"Yeah, no shit, right? That's exactly what I asked him, and he just sighs, like I'm wasting his time, and repeats the question. So I tell him 'no, I ain't a goddamn vegetarian, now are you gonna sell me this dog or what?' And there's this long pause, so long I check my phone to make sure one of us hasn't lost our connection, but then he says okay, says to meet him at a specific address at a certain time and to bring the cash, that if I'm even a minute late, no deal, turn back around because he won't be there. So, I'm like, okay, whatever, man, I'll be there. Just bring the dog."

"Where did he have you meet him?"

"In the middle of fucking Gary, of all places. Behind this 7–Eleven with more bullet holes in the front window than I could count."

"What time was this?"

"Two in the goddamn morning. In Gary. Behind a gas station."

"I'm honestly shocked you're even alive right now."

"Yeah, well, try telling that to me tomorrow."

"I will. And it'll still be true."

"Teddy, optimism gets people nowhere."

Ted held up his hand to cut him off. "Do you hear that?"

"Hear what?"

"Something. I don't know. Something banging." He leaned toward the room opening, focusing. Somewhere, mostly drowned by the deep freezer hum, he heard a noise.

"I think you're just drunk. My boy Teddy ain't used to drinking with the big boys no more, is that it?"

"Shut up. I'm serious. Someone's at the door."

Ted climbed up to his feet and eyed the revolver still on the floor and wondered if he should take it with him, then realized these were the thoughts of a lunatic. For one thing, the gun wasn't registered in his name. Ted had not once in his entire life conceived of registering for a firearm permit. Growing up in Hammond either gave you a great appreciation for guns or a great loathing for them. You couldn't even walk down to the corner store without the very real possibility of somebody sticking one in your face. It'd actually happened to him and Justin. Not just once, either. They learned not to leave the house with anything valuable in their possession unless they never wanted to see it again, because you never knew. Just looking at one in a movie or TV show sometimes made Ted nauseated. Some things a person couldn't get over.

Justin threw an empty PBR at Ted as he left the room. "Don't answer it! Goddammit, Teddy, come back here!"

Ted continued through the basement. The knocking wasn't coming from the front of the house, but the back door located at the top of the first set of stairs. The same way Ted had entered. He gave himself a brief once-over in case he looked like a man who had his best friend chained to a ship anchor, then opened the door. The sun was barely visible behind the trees ahead. A nice, cool breeze welcomed his return from the insanity downstairs.

Standing on the back porch was a small boy no older than nine or ten. He had a grin on his face and a dead rabbit in his arms.

ELEVEN

"HELLO! MY NAME IS DYLAN!" THE KID HELD OUT the dead rabbit by its ears. Fresh blood dripped down its carcass and splattered on the wooden porch. "That'll be twenty dollars, please!"

Ted stood in place and stared at the kid and his offering for a flat minute without responding. Internally he debated if Justin was right. Maybe he *had* had too much to drink. Sure. He'd used to pound away six-pack after six-pack back when he was twenty. But now? Shelly would kill him if she caught him pulling that kind of shit. She wasn't against drinking or anything like that. They often went out to the bar and got drunk together. But nothing close to *black-out* drunk. They had their limits. They played their lives mostly responsibly.

Regardless, he couldn't remember ever in his life getting drunk enough to experience hallucinations. Sure, Ted wasn't exactly sober right now. But he sure as shit wasn't hallucinating this kid. He was real, and so was the rabbit he held in his hand. The rabbit he desperately wanted Ted to accept.

"What...what is this?" The question not only referred to the rabbit and the kid's presence on the porch, but to the entire day. He wanted to grab the kid by his collar and shake him and demand explanations for everything fucked-up in his life. The drifting between him and Shelly. The girl at work. The inevitable consequences. Shelly packing her bags. Justin begging him to come over. A loaded gun in his hands. A kid with a dead rabbit.

The kid, Dylan, waved the rabbit back and forth from its ears. "The man. Where is the man?"

"Ju-Justin?"

Dylan nodded. "He needs this. I find it for him and he gives me twenty dollars. Then I go to the gas station and buy candy and Slurpees. I like the raspberry-flavored one but sometimes I mix all the flavors together. My friend Liam calls it a—"

"Suicide."

He nodded again, more enthusiastically. "Uh-huh, that's right. A suicide! Isn't that a weird name? I love them so much. All the flavors in your mouth at one time and it's like *BAM!* Makes my head hurt but in a good way. Sometimes it's okay for your head to hurt, right? But only sometimes. Hey, where is the man? Is he coming?"

"He's…uh…he's busy. I'm sorry."

Dylan shrugged. The kid didn't give a shit. "Okay. Then you pay me. Twenty dollars, please!" He tried to shove the rabbit in Ted's arms but he backed away. No way in hell was he touching that.

"No thanks. Not today. We're, uh, we're all set for right now."

The kid frowned. He refused to pull the dead rabbit away. Instead he pushed it forward again. "Twenty dollars, please!"

"I don't have any money. I'm sorry." Ted reached both

hands into his pants pockets and shrugged. He wasn't lying, either. He almost never walked around with cash these days. What was the point? Basically every place worth going to was equipped with a card swiper.

"But…" The kid held the rabbit over his head. Blood trickled onto his face. Ted grimaced and stepped away, watching the red drops stream down the kid's cheek. "This is for the man. All days. He wants animal. I want twenty dollars. Where is the man?"

"I'm—I'm sorry. He's busy. I have to go. I'm sorry."

Ted shut the door and tried to lock it—except the lock was still busted, so he just held it in place for a little while instead. He pressed his ear against the frame and listened. The kid still stood on the porch, shuffling his feet, saying something about twenty dollars under his breath. Then the porch wood creaked as he walked away, followed by rust whining as he opened and closed the fence gate.

Ted stormed back downstairs and found Justin on the mattress. Where else could he go? "What the fuck, man?"

Justin stared into his lap, refusing to make eye contact. "What?"

"You know what."

"Was that Dylan?"

"You mean, was that the child you apparently pay to bring you dead animals? Yes. Yes, it was."

"Well, where is it?"

"Where's what."

Justin finally lifted his head. Shame filled his eyes, but also desperation. "My food."

"Your food."

"You already said he brought it over, right? So where is it?"

"I told him to get the hell out of here."

His embarrassment evolved to fury. "You didn't pay him?"

"I am not going to pay a child for a dead rabbit so you can eat it. That's…that's crazy."

"He managed to find a rabbit?" Justin licked his lips, then realized what he was doing and covered his hand over his mouth.

"You actually eat that shit? This roadkill?"

"I can't control the craving. The craving controls me. That's what I've been trying to tell you."

"How often do you have him bringing you dead animals?"

"Whenever he finds them."

"Putting your parents' inheritance to good use, I see." Then an idea occurred to him. "Wait. How sure are you that these animals are already dead when he finds them? You don't think he's the one killing them, do you? Just so he can earn some extra money."

Justin shrugged. "I don't care how he comes across them. That's none of my business."

"You're pathetic."

"So shoot me then."

"Fuck you."

"No, fuck *you*." He pointed at the revolver Ted had left on the floor next to the deep freezer. "Shoot me. Shoot me shoot me fucking *shoot me*!"

Ted ran his hands through his hair and pulled from his skull, trying to rip off his scalp. The pain won and he released his grip. He couldn't do this. Not now, not ever.

He turned around and walked not just out of the basement, but out of the house. He got in his car and backed out of the gravel driveway and into the desolate alley behind Justin's house. Before driving away, he stared briefly at a pair of shoes hanging from a telephone wire and wondered if they'd once belonged to him. A faraway memory tried dragging him through its vortex but he waved it away. Fuck this place. He should have never come back here.

TWELVE

TED DROVE AROUND HAMMOND WITHOUT ANY REAL destination in mind. The beer seemed to widen and distort the shape of the road. It swirled his perception of reality and roughened the waves in his stomach. The car swerved. It hit nothing. The road was empty. Empty except for Ted. Every lane belonged to him and he greedily claimed them all.

He called Shelly, taking his eyes away from the road for far too long. When he looked back up he was seconds away from bashing into a tree. He jerked to the left and straightened out on the road. By the time he lifted the phone to his ear, the voicemail machine was already telling him to leave a message.

"*I'm coming! You hear that? I'm coming! You better fucking answer the door or I'm gonna knock it down, I swear to God! I swear to fucking God!*"

Going to her mother's house would be a mistake. He knew that. But there weren't many other places he could drive to. Back home, in their empty house? He couldn't be in that place by himself right now. That house was a house of pain. Every framed photograph. Every forgotten piece of clothing. Everything was a memory. Everything was a knife to the gut. Twist and push, twist and push.

It would take him about an hour to drive back to his mother-in-law's house. He could drive over, bang on the door until somebody answered, make sure Shelly was okay, then drive back to Justin's long before midnight.

But why did it matter that he make it back at midnight? Ted didn't buy into Justin's bullshit for a second. At least, he didn't want to. Regardless of what Ted believed, something clearly had happened to Justin since the last time they'd seen each other. The man was not well. Ted couldn't just abandon him down in the basement, chained to some goddamn *ship anchor* of all things. He still couldn't imagine how Justin had managed to get that thing from a boat to his house. His ribs were visible underneath his skin. He was a walking skeleton. No goddamn way could he have lifted an anchor up by himself. Would he have even been able to drive with one, or would it have dragged the bottom of his car against the road? Steel scraping against cement, sparks firing at whoever was unlucky enough to be driving behind him. The more Ted thought about the situation, the less any of it made sense.

He drove toward the highway onramp, intent on seeing Shelly no matter the costs. Justin had locked himself to that anchor. It wasn't Ted's fault that he was there all alone. Maybe by the time he made it back to Hammond, Justin would have come to his senses and realized what a whackjob he'd been today.

Emergency lights flashed and blinded him from up ahead. The road leading to the onramp had been blocked off by orange cones and several police cars. A line of civilian cars were backed up halfway down the street.

"Oh, fuck."

It was a DUI checkpoint. Of all the goddamn times. Ted couldn't even get mad. It made sense in a wicked, evil sort of way. Destiny wagging its middle finger down at him and spitting in his face and telling him he wasn't going anywhere.

Ted served into a McDonald's before the checkpoint could trap him. The sight of the drive-thru menu made his mouth water. Despite the dead rabbit shoved in his face not even a half hour ago, he still found his stomach grumbling for something to eat. He hadn't had anything since yesterday. He was going to eat lunch with Justin earlier, but Justin ended up eating both of their burgers, leaving Ted with a soda sea of soggy french fries to scavenge from linoleum. Beer resided in his stomach and nothing else. He'd gone down this route before and it always led to a night of painful vomiting. Meat and carbohydrates were the only effective antidotes.

The speaker shouted for him to tell it his order. He asked for two double cheeseburgers, then paused, hating himself for saying what he was about to say but knowing realistically he had little choice, and requested ten additional burgers.

"No pickles, please."

THIRTEEN

J USTIN LOOKED DEAD BY THE TIME TED MADE IT BACK down to the basement. He'd managed to crawl a good two feet past the mattress before surrendering to the weight of the anchor. He lay sprawled out on the cement, facedown, arm extended toward the deep freezer. He'd been after the revolver Ted abandoned on the floor. He hadn't even come close to reaching it.

For good measure, Ted still kicked it farther away as he sat down against the deep freezer. The basement smelled worse than before he left. He spotted a puddle of urine in the far corner of the room, behind the mattress and ship anchor. The padlock key felt heavy in Ted's pocket and another wave of shame washed over him.

He tried nudging Justin awake but the man wouldn't budge, so he unwrapped one of the burgers and held it next to his face like it was a smelling salt. A second passed and Justin stirred awake.

"Hungry. So hungry."

He lifted his head from the floor and chomped a bite of the burger from Ted's hand. Ted flinched, afraid he might lose a finger. He'd come awfully close.

Justin talked as he chewed. "You came back."

"Yeah."

"Meat. You brought meat." He sat up and grabbed the burger with both hands and dived into it. A drowning victim mercifully washed onto land. "Oh, you beautiful motherfucker. You came back and you brought *meat*."

Ted took two burgers out of the bag and pushed the rest of the bag toward the mattress. "There's nine more in there for you. Go nuts."

Justin peeked into the bag then looked up at him like he was in love. "I could kiss you right now. I could kiss you right on that sexy little butthole of yours."

"I…I'd prefer you didn't."

"You came back!"

"I couldn't just leave you like this."

"You brought meat!"

"Well. It's better than roadkill, I imagine."

"There is literally no difference."

"I'm…I'm sure there is."

Ted studied his food a little longer than he desired before biting into it. If he ever wanted to go on a diet, Justin would be an ideal roommate. With just a few words he could squash the hunger of a man dying from starvation.

Ted sipped from his McDonald's fountain drink. "I guess you ought to finish your story."

Justin smiled, hopeful. "You want to hear the rest?"

"I'm here, aren't I?"

"That you are, brother. That you are."

"So you bought a dog on Craigslist. Because you wanted to be a dogfighter."

"Dogman."

"Excuse me?"

"Someone who trains a dog to fight, they're called dogmen. I'm not the one fighting dogs, so why would I be a dogfighter?"

"Okay, fine. You wanted to be a dogman, then."

He nodded. "That was the goal, correct."

"Well, what happened with the dog?"

"Insert quotation marks around the word *dog*."

"What?"

"So the guy wants to meet late as fuck behind that 7-Eleven, right? The one clear out in goddamn Gary. *Gary.*"

"The chances of survival do not sound promising."

"Yeah, no shit, right? So I get there right on the fucking dot, and there's this big white van already parked, just waiting. The kind of van that pops up in your head when I tell you to picture a rape van. This thing was the king of rape vans. Even had a broken taillight. So stereotypical, right? I figure, well shit, that must be the guy, and run up to him like he's peddling ice cream. He rolls the window down not even halfway, and it's so fucking dark, I can't see his face. I suddenly start thinking oh shit, this might be a trap, what if he shoves a gun out the window and blows my brains out? But he just says, in this real deep, sick voice, 'Slide the money through.' And I'm standing outside the van, froze-up, and I tell him, 'Wait, where's this dog?' And he says, 'The animal is in the back. Slide the money through the window or leave.' But I'm still stuck, because what if I give him the money and he just books it? But what if I piss him off and he leaves anyway, and I miss out on one of the best fightin' dogs ever bred? I mean, it was only three hundred, so I figured fuck it, life's nothing but a gamble, right? I hand him the money and he says, 'The back is unlocked. Take the animal and never contact me again.'"

"Sounds like a shady individual."

"No fucking shit. So I go and open the back and there's this huge kennel just sitting there, but it ain't empty, there's something fucking angry inside, trying to get out, clawing at the cage, biting the wiring, all that shit, and I'm standing there thinking holy shit, this thing is going to make me so much money."

"Instead of 'holy shit, this thing is going to rip my throat out the first chance it gets'?"

"I ain't never been much for hindsight."

Ted looked at the ship anchor and laughed. "I can see that."

"You're a dick." Justin cleared his throat, sipped his drink. "So, I drag it out of the van and dude, this thing was fucking heavy, okay? I couldn't even lift it, the kennel dropped straight to the ground and I had to push it through the dirt to my own car. The whole time, whatever's inside it is going apeshit, growling and snarling and clawing. I have to lay down both my back seats to get it into my trunk, and the whole time I'm driving home the back of my car is so low it's a miracle nothing scraped against the road. The longer I drive, the louder it whines. Maybe it's hungry, I start thinking, and realize I don't even have dog food at my house. I haven't even researched how to properly train a dog to fight, but I mean, it's not that big of an issue, the way this dog sounds, I won't need to train it, it'll need to train me."

"What does that even mean?"

Justin thought about it and shrugged. "I don't know. But it sounded cool, didn't it?"

"Sure."

"So I stop off at McDonald's,"—he chuckled and raised his burger in salute—"and I pick up a couple of these very same McDoubles or whatever the fuck, and just kind of... squish the shit through the holes in the crate, hoping like hell the thing doesn't bite off one of my fingers."

"Then you'd be Nine-Fingered Justin."

"Doesn't have the same ring as No Dick Rick. Hey, maybe that's how he lost his dick."

"By stuffing it through a scary crate and letting some rabid dog bite it off?" Ted tried to visualize the scene and immediately regretted it. "Yeah. You're probably right."

"Seems odd that he would still be involved with dog-fighting after that, though."

"Nothing will get in the way of his passion?"

Justin shrugged and unwrapped a new burger from the bag. "Now, I'm feeding this thing, right? Me in the front seat and the crate or kennel or whatever's in the back. And I'm trying to get a good look at the fucker, because at this point I still haven't really *seen* the thing. I'm just taking the guy's word for it that what I have is a dog and not some baby bear."

"A cub."

Justin paused and sneered. "Excuse me?"

"A baby bear is called a cub."

"Fuck that. I ain't calling no baby bear a cub."

"Typical Sox fan, rejecting the dictionary."

"Yeah, go fuck yourself. Anyway, now, this...this *thing*. I get out my phone and I try to use the screen as a flashlight to see inside, because the sounds it's making as it eats... they're legitimately scaring me. But as I raise my phone toward it, all of a sudden the thing inside starts screaming— no, not screaming. *Howling.*"

"Like a werewolf, right?"

"Exactly right."

"Justin. There's no—"

"So the howling scares me so much I end up jumping and dropping my phone. I figure, all right, fuck this, it ain't the place to start investigating big scary dogs. I head home, the whole time this fucking thing is going crazy in the back. I won't lie. A part of me begged to just pull over and push the kennel out on the street. Get rid of it while I still could. But…I did just pay three hundred dollars for it. Can you imagine throwing three hundred dollars out of your car just because?"

"Money doesn't howl, though."

"Maybe you just aren't listening hard enough."

"That…doesn't make any sense."

Justin balled up a couple empty wrappers and tossed them at the wall. "So, I pull up behind the house and I just leave the kennel inside the car and go inside and gulp down a beer, I'm shaking so much I can barely hold the can. Just trying to pump myself up enough to go back out there and bring it inside. But there was something about the way it kept growling on the drive over that scared me to death. So, I drank three more beers until I was too stupid to give a shit, and I dragged that motherfucker into my house, down here into the basement, since there was no way in hell I was gonna get it upstairs, and I'm just sitting on the floor, Indian-style, across from the crate, staring at whatever fucking thing I just bought. Because, you know, this is the first time I get a chance to see it with light. And, uh—"

"What did you see?"

"Well, it wasn't no fucking dog, that's for sure."

"Okay, and…?"

"It's hard to describe now. Especially since I was kinda

drunk at the time."

"You're drunk now, too."

"So fucking what? What are you trying to say?"

Ted shrugged. "I don't know. Seems like maybe you're able to remember drunken memories better when you're drunk. Like, the alcohol opens up forgotten doors."

Justin studied him for a second then burst out laughing. "Yeah, and I'm the one who's drunk. Jesus Christ, Teddy."

"I may have had a bit too much tonight."

"Well sober up for fuck's sake. I can't have you missing and shooting me in the dick and turning me into a Rick."

"I'm not gonna shoot—"

Justin held up his hand and shushed him. "But try to imagine a wolf, okay? Only the wolf's on steroids and its father might be a bear."

"Do you mean a cub?"

"No, motherfucker. I mean a *bear*."

"And it fit inside of a dog crate?"

"It was a really big crate, okay? And even then I'm not sure how anybody got it inside."

"What did you do?"

"I, uh, opened it."

"And was it happy to see you?"

Justin laughed, but not out of humor, more like how the survivor of a great tragedy might laugh while still in shock. "Man, as soon as my finger slid the goddamn lock off, the thing was snapping at me like I was the source of everything wrong in its life."

"Well, you *were* planning on making it fight to the death with other dogs."

"Yeah, but he didn't know that. Shit. So, I open it open and it starts snapping at me and charging. I turned and ran, screaming and begging it to be a nice doggy, *please be a nice little doggy, please please please*, but that thing was pissed at the world, man, I tell ya, there was no stopping it. I booked it into the bathroom, but the fucking thing bit into my calf at the last second. I managed to shake it off and close the door and lock it before—"

"Why did you lock it?"

"What?"

"Did the dog have opposable thumbs?"

"You weren't there, motherfucker. It was scary."

"It bit you on the leg?"

"Yeah."

"Let me see."

"Let you see *what*?"

Ted pointed at his leg. "It must've left a scar behind or something, right?"

Justin grinned. "All this time, you still don't believe a word I got to say. Do you?"

Of course he didn't, but Ted wasn't about to admit it. "I just want to see where it bit you."

"Yeah, all right, sure."

Justin rolled on his stomach and stuck his left leg out toward him. Ted scooted forward and slowly rolled the pants leg up.

Justin flinched. "Careful, goddammit."

"Sorry."

Ted practiced extra caution as he progressed the pants leg up his calf. A few inches from his ankle, Justin's skin ceased its cadaverous pigmentation and drastically darkened. His calf was black and red and covered in half-opened scabs.

Ted gasped and backed away. "Holy shit. That's really

infected."

"Yeah."

"You need to go to the hospital. That…that isn't good, Justin."

"You think I don't know that?" Justin turned around and sat up, leaving his pants rolled and his calf exposed. He pointed at the wound. "You think I don't know what they'll tell me when I go in? You think I don't know it's gonna need to be cut off? Oh, I know, brother, and believe me, I've thought about going in and getting it taken care of. Oh yes, I've thought about it. And I was going to, too. But shit got in the way, and here we are. But come midnight, I don't transform, you don't shoot me, first stop we'll make is the hospital, I swear to Christ. I'll even bring my own machete for them to use. 'Chop it off, doc. Chop it off and fuckin' *burn it*.'"

Ted shook his head, amazed. "I don't understand how the infection hasn't spread."

Justin laughed so loud he practically howled. "Oh, it spread, all right. Believe me right here and now. It spread. It spread *everywhere*."

FOURTEEN

"SO I LOCK MYSELF IN THE BATHROOM AND THE DOG or whatever the fuck it is starts, like, furiously scratching at the door, trying to claw its way through the wood, trying to catch its supper, and—"

"Wouldn't you be dessert?"

"What?"

Ted didn't even know why he'd opened his mouth. "If it already ate McDonald's on the way over, wouldn't that have been its supper? So you'd be the dessert, right?"

Justin paused, maybe waiting for a punch line that didn't exist. "What the hell is wrong with you?"

"I don't know."

"Anyway." He shook his head like an annoyed parent. "The dog's trying to get into the bathroom, and I'm in there, leg bleeding like a motherfucker, oh my God, you have no idea how much it hurt, I legit thought I was going to pass out from the pain, and I'm desperately going through all the cabinets in there trying to find something—*anything*—that might help me defend myself if—no, *when*—this fucking animal breaks through the door."

"Too bad you didn't have the gun back then." Ted lifted the revolver, in case Justin had somehow forgotten it existed, then set it back down on the floor.

"Yeah, no shit. I fucking *wish* I'd had that on me at the time. But that wasn't the case. What *was* the case was this: I'd locked myself in a bathroom, and I was bleeding badly. A dog or some shit was trying to kill me. If I didn't think of something soon, the dog would succeed. Let me tell you right now, Teddy: there was no fucking way I was gonna be some shithead dog's dinner."

"Dessert."

"Shut the fuck up."

"I'm sorry."

Ted unwrapped his second burger. Justin had already eaten the ten he'd gotten him. Ted could hardly believe it. The man didn't possess an ounce of fat on him. Where did all the food go? How could he devour ten cheeseburgers in one sitting without exploding?

Justin watched Ted eat his second burger with hunger in his eyes. Ted avoided eye contact while he ate. It was very awkward.

Justin licked his lips and continued. "I didn't have a gun in that bathroom, but I did have some scissors."

"Not exactly the same thing."

"Not at all, but they were still sharp as hell and could easily cause some major damage. I use them to trim my nose hairs, and trust me, the slightest nick will have you bleeding for hours."

"Were you going to trim the dog's nose hairs?"

"I was going to shove it through the fucker's throat."

"And did you?"

"Nah. It eventually got tired of scratching the door and gave up, went off to explore the rest of the house. I stayed in the bathroom for a couple hours, just sitting on the toilet, both hands clutching the scissors, too afraid to even breathe much less *move*. The whole time I can hear it roaming around the house and tearing into things and knocking shit down and howling. It sounded like it was losing its mind. At least I know I was."

"What—losing your mind?"

He smirked and tapped the side of his skull with his fist. "Still ain't found it, either."

Justin picked up his fountain drink and sucked on the straw, realized it was empty, and threw it in the growing pile of trash at the wall opposite of the mattress. He belched as if he hadn't just drank oxygen.

"I started to get afraid that maybe the dog-thing would never rest, that it'd keep destroying the house until I either opened the door and offered myself or died from thirst or starvation or old age or whatever came to claim me first. Now, I ain't Elvis—"

Ted gave him a double-take. "You're not?"

Justin shook his head, serious. "No, sir. I'm far more handsome than that talentless prick."

"Harsh thing to say about a dead man."

He laughed. "Like I give a shit. I'll be joining him here in a few hours, anyway."

"Oh, that's right."

"But where him and I differ is, there's no goddamn way I'm dying on some toilet. So—"

"There's definitely more nobility in dying chained to a ship anchor."

Justin opened his mouth wide in preparation for a scream and bit his fist to muffle the sound. He grimaced and wiped saliva off his hand. "A few hours pass. I'm feeling weak. My leg's bleeding and throbbing. Yeah, I washed it under the bathtub faucet and covered the wound with a bandage, but that didn't do much to stop the pain. There's no way I can sit on the toilet much longer. So I say screw it. If I'm gonna die, I'm gonna go out fighting. I take my scissors and I open the door and peek my head through the crack and look around, but I'm just being overly cautious because I can hear the motherfucker upstairs in the kitchen, its paws thumping against the floor. I creep up the steps, almost excited about the prospect of slicing this thing's throat, the pain in my leg's so great I'm convinced the only medicine worth taking right then is revenge. I want to bathe in this bitch's blood and turn its hide into a rug. I can picture it so carefully, it's crazy. I get halfway up the steps and I'm high enough to peek through the bottom of the railing and there it is, in the middle of the kitchen, feasting on a mess of trash it's spread after tipping over the can. I'm staring at this new animal—this new *thing*—that I've bought off Craigslist, this *creature* that ain't no dog, ain't no wolf, ain't no thing I've ever seen in my goddamn life, and suddenly all that heroism drains from my body and I can't move, I'm frozen, and all I want to do is get as fucking far away as possible, but I can't, I can't do anything but stand and watch this thing eat. Then it notices me, of course it notices me. Maybe it hears me breathing or maybe it smells my fear, who knows. Does fear have a smell?"

"I—I don't know."

"Yeah, me neither. But all I *do* know is that one second it's chowing down on some old, half-eaten chicken leg I'd thrown away a week ago—yeah, I know, my fault for forgetting to take out the trash—and the next second, it stops eating and starts snarling loud and vicious and lifting up its head and stares me down—like, making full eye contact, and my legs start moving before my brain can catch up with what's exactly happening. I can hear the thing rushing down the steps after me as I bolt out of the back door and it crashes through the screen, determined to tear me a new asshole. I flee straight across the back porch and just kind of leap over the ledge, thinking I'll land on my feet and keep running, you know, like someone would do in a movie, all cool as fuck, except of course I tripped on the ledge and landed on my face, successfully reawakening the wound in my leg. Instantly it soaks through my latest bandage. Thankfully, the dog-thing didn't seem to notice I'd fallen, maybe it'd built up too much momentum coming after me, because it also jumped off the porch, only it made a successful landing, and it didn't even think twice about turning around, it just kept running down the alley, toward who the fuck knows. Once I realized I wasn't being eaten, after all, I scrambled back inside the house and locked all the doors and passed out the moment I made it to bed."

"What happened to the dog?"

Justin shrugged. "Hell if I know."

"It didn't come back?"

"I haven't seen it since that night."

"Did you call somebody? Like animal control or something?"

"And tell them what?" Justin mimed his hand into a telephone and pressed it against his ear. "'Oh yes, hello, the dog I bought to use in fights just bit me and ran away. Also, it's actually not a dog. It's some kind of monster from Hell and it's going to kill us all.'" He hung up the fake phone. "Get real, man."

"Yeah. That's exactly what you should have said."

"Don't be ridiculous."

"What if it attacked somebody else?"

Justin tried to act like the thought had never occurred to him before, but it was clear in his eyes burden weighed heavily inside him. "Hopefully they were faster than I was."

Ted considered pressing the issue, but gave up. There was no point in continuing to make him feel bad. They couldn't go back in time and prevent the rabid dog from escaping. What was done was done.

Justin cleared his throat. "I'm thinking we could both use some more beer. What do you say?"

"Yeah. I think maybe you're right."

Ted stood and leaned against the deep freezer as the tingling sensation in his legs faded. Justin pointed at the mountain of trash at the end of the room. "Uh, before you go, can you be a pal and hand me that empty McDonald's cup? I gotta pee."

FIFTEEN

THERE WAS ONLY ONE SIX-PACK OF PBR LEFT IN the fridge. Ted remembered when he first opened it earlier that afternoon. It had looked so full. What happened after the next six beers were gone? They would have nothing left. The thought depressed him more than he figured was rational.

On the way down, he stopped in the basement bathroom to relieve himself. He crouched next to the door after he finished and studied the scratched wood. The clawmarks were thick, deep. One hell of a big dog had tried getting through. One hell of a big something.

The McDonald's cup rested next to the mattress. The shadow of Justin's urine filled a quarter of the container. Ted felt a weird, compelling urge to kick it. Nothing seemed to be in his control today—hell, who was he kidding, nothing had been in his control for a very long time—and possessing the ability to knock over a pee cup just because he wanted to made him feel good inside. Or maybe that was the beer talking. He sat down before the urge won and distributed the beers between him and Justin.

Ted popped the tab on one and licked the foam. "So, you ran back inside and locked the door. Then what? Why didn't you go to the hospital? How were you even able to walk?"

Justin drank a good while before answering. "Well, at the time, I was too scared to go back outside. If I wanted to leave, I'd have to make it from my back door to my car. Not exactly the shortest walk, right? What if the thing was out in my yard, or still in the alley, just waiting to see if I was stupid enough to show my face again? As soon as I step outside, *bam,* it lunges at me."

"Didn't you say you saw it run down the alley, though?"

"Doesn't mean it didn't turn around and return to the house once it realized I'd never left. No. It seemed smarter to just wait inside for a while, wait for everything to cool down. Plus, you know, I was getting pretty goddamn woozy. The whole room was spinning, which made sense considering how much blood I'd lost. And my wound was *still* bleeding, so I took the now soaked bandage off, washed it again, and wrapped it with a clean cloth, then collapsed on my mattress and passed out. I woke up the next day screaming. I don't mean I woke up and started screaming. It was more like I woke up and I'd already been screaming for a good long while. Been screaming so long and hard that my throat was sore as shit. My leg fucking *throbbed,* dude. You got no fuckin' idea how much it hurt. I took a long, hot shower and thought about my predicament. I could go to the hospital and have it looked at, but what if they started asking a bunch of questions? Would they know I'd been trying to train a dog to fight?"

"How would they have known that unless you told them?"

"I don't know. You weren't fucking there. Don't judge me, asshole. At the time, I was convinced they'd be able to tell. Hell, maybe I was just paranoid."

"There's no *maybe* about it." Ted pointed his beer at him. "People get bitten by dogs all the time. They don't have to prove that they weren't involved in dogfighting. They just get patched up and sent on their way. You could have told them you were walking down the street and some stray came at you."

"Well, okay, but also, there was another reason I wanted to avoid the hospital."

"Your fear of needles?"

Justin laughed, scratching the hives on his face. "Remember, Jessica works there? What if I ran into her?"

"So what?"

"That'd be really embarrassing. I don't think I would have been able to handle letting her see me in such a distraught state."

"It's…it's her job to see people in distraught states. She's a nurse."

"Yeah, but, like, it's different with me. We've fucked."

"Like over fifteen years ago."

"Still, though. Man. No. I can't do it, okay? I just can't. I still think about her sometimes."

Ted sighed. "Okay. I get it. You were freaked out and weren't thinking clearly." He stared at the anchor and chains imprisoning Justin in the bedroom and debated revising his use of the word "weren't", but decided against it. "Continue the story. Did you at least contact the psychopath who sold you the dog?"

Justin nodded and took his time elaborating. "Of course I called him. After I got out of the shower and looked at my bite, that's the first thing I did. But did he answer?" He laughed. "What the fuck do you think? Would *you* have?"

"I don't think I would have sold a monster dog on

Craigslist to begin with."

"I'm sure that guy once thought the same thing. Life's full of surprises, ain't it?"

Ted looked around the room—at the empty beer cans and the dirty mattress and the ship anchor and the chains—and nodded. "I suppose so."

"But yeah. I tried looking him up on Craigslist, but his account had been deleted. Removed from existence, like it'd never been there to begin with. Wiped like a hacker surrounded by sirens. Can't say I was surprise. I think I knew the moment he drove away in his van that I'd never see him again. The man fled the 7-Eleven like he'd just committed a murder."

"Maybe you could have—"

"—and even if I *did* manage to contact him, what would I say? He'd been pretty up front in what he was advertising: a killing machine. That's what I paid him for. Realistically, to say I hadn't gotten my money's worth would be a lie, if you really think about it."

"I—I guess that's true. But still. He could have given you a warning that it'd go on a rampage the moment you got him home. Usually when you buy a dog, the seller provides a list of personal instructions about diet and caring for the animal. To just drop the thing off and drive away is very unprofessional."

Justin scratched his head. "Well, I mean, like, I found him on Craigslist and we met behind a 7-Eleven. Wasn't like he'd ever shown any signs of professionalism."

"Yeah. I don't think anything professional has ever occurred on the property of a 7-Eleven."

"Right. So, too afraid to go to a hospital, I googled how to treat a dog bite, even though I suspected what had bitten me wasn't exactly a dog, but it was close enough. I couldn't exactly google 'how to treat a bite from a big scary-ass monster I bought off Craigslist', now could I?"

"No. But now I'm interested in what would pop up."

Ted stretched his legs forward and arched his back so he could fit his hand into his pocket and pulled out his phone. Any excuse to check for a missed text from Shelly. Still nothing. At this point, he fully realized he was entertaining a delusion. She wasn't planning on texting him back, not any time soon. Maybe not ever again. She meant what she said. A break was a break. Could he ever accept that? It seemed unlikely. He didn't know what life was supposed to be without his wife at his side. What was the point?

He opened up Safari to google Justin's ridiculous yet accurate question. No signal. This basement was a death box. The Internet. Justin. Hell, even Ted. Everything in here wanted to die.

He set the phone on the floor next to the revolver and stared at the two, side-by-side. Which would be more satisfying—shooting himself, or shooting the phone? Maybe he could do both. Justin said it was loaded with two bullets. One for the phone, the other for Ted. Let Justin starve to death chained to his stupid anchor. Sure. Why not? He'd brought this upon himself. But then again, hadn't Ted done the same?

"Well?" Justin leaned forward in anticipation. "What did it say?"

"That your network is currently unavailable."

"Dude. It's a basement. What did you expect?"

Ted shrugged. "I typically don't spend my evenings in basements. Especially with werewolves."

Justin grinned and slapped his thigh. "So you believe

me then!"

"Uh…no. I was joking."

"Oh, you fucking dick."

"I'm sorry." Ted popped the tab on his last beer. "But so far, you haven't exactly given me a reason to believe."

"Well, if you weren't constantly fucking interrupting me—"

"You're right, you're right. I'm sorry. Go ahead. Talk. I won't interrupt you again." Ted tried to prevent a laugh from escaping, but it was too late. Too much beer, maybe. Too much everything.

Justin shook his head, rubbing his temples. "Some fucking people, I swear to God…"

Ted leaned his head against the deep freezer and closed his eyes. "I'm sorry. I'm drunk."

"Then stop drinking!"

"But you keep giving them to me."

"I can't even get up. What are you talking about?"

"Oh. Right." Ted belched. "Just tell me what happened next. The dog bites you, you fall asleep, wake up, shower, you can't contact the Craigslist dude, so then what? How do you go from 'guy with a dog bite' to 'werewolf asking his friend to shoot him in the heart'?"

"Well, the thing is…"

SIXTEEN

"THE DAY THAT I WAS SUPPOSED TO PICK UP THE dog—back then, I was still thinking of it as a dog, which I guess seems like a real dumbass move on my part now that I know what I know, kind of like the family who moves into a haunted house and they still think of their house as a *house* even after worms spill from the outlets and some ghost molests their daughter or whatever the fuck—anyway, I'd just gotten done talking with the guy from Craigslist, and oh man, I was so friggin' excited, I couldn't keep it a secret, there was no way. I would have exploded. So I called up Rick and said, 'Hey, No-Dick'—"

"No you didn't."

"—okay, I didn't *actually* call him 'No-Dick'. I'm insane, sure, but I'm not fucking *crazy*, right? No, I said, 'Hey, Rick, guess what your boy just picked up?' And he responded with some smartass comment like, 'I don't know, your boyfriend's dick?' You know, like something you would probably say."

"I'm not homophobic."

"You've made your share of gay jokes. Don't even fucking play, bro."

"Maybe when I was younger, sure, but…"

"Nobody gives a shit. What I'm saying is—he caught

me off guard with that kind of answer, so I said back, 'Says the guy without one,' and holy shit, Teddy, as soon as the words left my mouth I swear to God, I felt my own dick retreat inside of me. I mean, that's always been unspoken territory—a no-fly zone—and there I was, running my mouth like I was King Shit of Fuck Town."

"I'm surprised you're alive right now to tell me about it."

"But he didn't say shit about it. Just kind of went quiet for a while and sighed and when he finally did respond, you could tell I'd kind of hurt him. He asked me what I wanted, in this real quiet tone, and I said, 'I just bought the biggest, meanest motherfucking dog in the world, and it is going to kill every other dog at the fight next weekend,' which I guess was enough of a change of topic for him to forget what I'd said—or, at least, *pretend* to forget what I'd said—because he perks right the hell up and matches my excitement. Asks me where I managed to get a dog, and I… maybe kind of exaggerated the truth."

"Exaggerated how?"

"I told him I'd driven over to Detroit and bought it from a guy connected to the Mafia. That the dog used to fight in New York where all the best, bloodiest fights go down. Some kinda shit like that."

"So you lied."

"Yeah." He nodded. "I lied."

"And he believed you?"

"Has No-Dick Rick ever struck you as a man of great intelligence?"

"Valid point."

"He asks if the dog will be ready by next weekend to compete, and I give him some shit like, 'Rick, this dog would be ready tonight if there was a fight going on.' And of course he says, 'Actually, there's a small little fight going down in an hour.' But, you know, I don't actually have the thing in my possession at the time, so I tell him I was kidding, that I need another week for the dog to get comfortable in my company, for me to show it who's the master in our relationship."

Ted snickered. "Relationship?"

"Or whatever you'd call it. I don't know." Justin grimaced. "Don't even try suggesting I was planning on fucking the dog. I know that's what you're thinking."

"I was thinking no such thing."

"You're a terrible liar. Also, you're not okay with gay jokes, but when it comes to bestiality jokes, that's totally cool?"

"I wasn't suggesting you were going to fuck the dog! Holy shit."

Justin stared at Ted, extremely serious, for a solid thirty seconds before he burst out laughing. "I'm just fuckin' with ya, Teddy. I was totally going to make sweet love to that pooch."

"Oh, shut up."

Justin giggled and continued. "So I tell Rick to give us a week and me and the dog should be ready to brawl. He asks if I'm sure and I tell him hell yeah I'm sure. He says 'all right' and tells me he's gonna make a phone call and schedule my name for one of the big fights—that is, if my dog can handle it. 'My dog will kill any motherfucker you put in front of it,' I tell him, and he laughs and tells me he'll try to get me into the main event, the big fucking showdown. Says he knows the guy who's fighting next week and it just so happens his opponent had to make a last-minute cancellation, and he didn't think the spot had been filled yet. Says if these dogmen hate one thing, it's a cancelled fight. These people pump themselves up all week for these fights, and to show up to…to *nothing* is like a dogfighter's equivalent to blue balls."

The situation started sinking in. "So, you had a fight scheduled despite the fact that you didn't actually have the dog yet. And when you *did* pick up the dog, it escaped almost immediately."

Justin nodded. "That's correct."

"And how did No-Dick take the news when you called and canceled the fight?"

"Your first mistake is assuming I was smart enough to call him and cancel it."

"What? You didn't call?"

"Excuse me for having bigger things on my mind. I spent that whole week just laying around depressed, getting drunk and cleaning the bite on my leg. It got…pretty bad. Not only was the pain immense, but I'd started seeing things, too. Like, fuckin' hallucinating. Weird shadows and bugs on the wall. Shit like that. And I kept hearing this… this *howling*, like twenty-four-fuckin'-seven, dude. Couldn't get it out of my ears. It wasn't real, at least I don't think it was, but who really knows, right? Hell, maybe I was the one making the noise. But yeah, there was one day when I was particularly drunk that I convinced myself it would need to be amputated—my leg—but like I said, no fuckin' way was I going to the hospital—could you imagine Jessica getting to cut off my leg? she'd have the time of her life—so I started googling how to perform an amputation at home. DIY as a motherfucker."

"Jesus."

"The images that came up were not, uh, very encouraging. Anyway, thankfully I fell asleep before I could actually grow the balls to go through with it, and by the time I woke up, I was sober enough to realize what a stupid fucking idea that was."

Ted studied the near-empty can of PBR in his lap. "Maybe alcohol isn't our friend, after all."

"Maybe not."

"So what happened the next weekend when you didn't have a dog to fight?"

"Okay, so first of all, I hadn't even realized a week had already passed. Time was moving at a weird pace. My head was on fire and—"

"Did you have a fever?"

"What?"

"A fever. If your head was on fire—"

"Like I own a fuckin' thermometer. Get real, son."

"Your mom didn't have one here?"

"Okay, so maybe I didn't think to look for one. Not like the thermometer wouldn't have told me something I didn't already fucking know, though. No shit I had a fever. I felt like my brain was melting against my skull. I spent that whole week going from freezing to burning up within seconds. My cell phone died and I didn't have the energy to charge it. Come Sunday, I was starting to feel a little bit more alive, but it still didn't register in my head what was supposed to happen the day before. It just felt like any other day, minus the feeling that I was on the verge of death."

"Those are always good days."

"So the door knocks and all of a sudden it hits me. What today is. What yesterday was. And I think oh shit. There's no way in hell I'm answering that. But as it turns out, I don't gotta, because these crazy sons of bitches kick it in, break off the lock, the knob, all that shit. And here I am, downstairs on the couch, watching TV in my underwear. Totally not ready for whatever's about to go down."

"Oh, yeah. I saw the door earlier. They really messed it up."

"That ain't all they messed up."

"They beat on you?"

"Well, when they first barged in, they ran directly upstairs, because I guess they're thinking what kind of creepy motherfucker hangs out in a basement in the middle of the afternoon? I don't know. But I did use this opportunity to gracefully sneak out the back door while they searched for me upstairs. I get about two feet on the porch—still in my underwear, mind you—when some big fuckin' goon who'd been waiting outside snatches me and drags me back into the house. I scream and kick but it's no use. This is Hammond. People are more concerned when they *aren't* hearing strangers screaming from a distance."

"I'm so glad I don't live in this shit-ass town anymore."

"I wish I could've done the same."

"What was stopping you?"

"All the bullshit that holds this world together." He paused before continuing, rubbing the target drawn on his chest. "So, this savage—the one who grabbed me out on the porch—he drags me upstairs with the rest of his fuckboys. In total, there's three or four of them. Hard to exactly remember now, but yeah, they're all assholes who frequent the dog fights. One of them, his name's Donny, he's basically the one in charge of recording the bets and scheduling matches. The one guy you don't wanna piss off, and of course I've gone and done exactly that."

"You know." Ted leaned forward and readjusted the position of his legs. "I'm kind of surprised at how organized dogfighting actually is. I guess, in my head, I figured people just showed at random spots and threw their dogs against other dogs and whoever's dog was still alive won. I never would have thought opponents would be scheduled weeks in advance."

"Well, sure. Some dogfighting is like what you just said. Street fights and shit. Brawls to squash beefs. But that's not what I got my dumb ass involved in. No-Dick, he don't fuck around with your normal variety thug. He socializes with the top-quality motherfuckers who pride themselves on the highest levels of professionalism. I'm not talking mafia. Not like that. Just...people who don't fuck around, you know? People you don't want to make commitments to and then fail to deliver unless you're cool with walking around with a limp for the rest of your sorry-ass life, if you're even that lucky."

"Why would anybody possibly be cool with that?"

"I don't know. Maybe there's some kind of limp fetish out there. People are into some kinky stuff."

"You could just fake it."

"Fake it?"

"The limp."

Justin pointed at him. "Clearly you are not an *authentic* limp fetishist, my friend."

Ted lowered his head, caught red-handed, too drunk to know whether this was a real reason to be ashamed. "I'm sorry."

Justin belched and tossed an empty can of PBR across the room and cracked his knuckles, settling into the story. "So, they make me sit down at my kitchen table, right? Donny, the dude in charge of the fights, he sits across from me, and his scumbag friends kind of linger behind me in case I try to split, which—don't get me wrong—is exactly what I'm thinking about doing right about now. So would you, put in the same situation."

"I don't think I would be in that kind of situation."

"*Nobody* thinks they'd be in that kind of situation until they're in it. Shit like that you can't predict. It just happens, and you gotta deal with it the best you can."

"And how did you deal with it?"

"Well. I wasn't really given no choice. I knew if I made one wrong move, one of the goons behind me wouldn't hesitate in bashing my skull in. So I just sat at the table and waited for Donny to do whatever it was he was gonna do."

"What did he do?"

"First, he asks me if I know what day it is, and yeah, for one quick second I start thinking maybe I should act like I think it's only Friday. Maybe he'll take it easy on me if I'm just a retard who was never taught the days of the week. But I get a feeling that if I try this tactic, he'll just waste me right there in the kitchen for further wasting his time. So I tell him yeah, I know what day it is, and he asks me if I knew what yesterday was, and I tell him yeah, I know what yesterday was, and he says, 'Well, I thought maybe you done forgot, since nobody seen your pretty little face all night.' So I tell him the same shit I just got through telling you. That the goddamn dog bit me and escaped out the back door. Even show him my calf so he knows I ain't making shit up. He asks me to peel off the bandage, so I do, and he gestures for me to prop the leg up on the table so he can get a good look. I lean back in the chair and plop my leg up." Justin stretched out his wounded leg again for emphasis, pointing at the infected horror show swallowing his calf. "And he stands up and leans over it, really inspecting the damage, then...then this motherfucker sticks his finger into it."

"Into...what?"

"Into my fucking bite wound, man."

"Oh my God." Ted forced his mouth shut in case he vomited, which suddenly felt like a real possibility.

"He just pokes his index finger through like it's nothing. Up to his fuckin' knuckle, dude. Like, I can almost feel his fingertip rubbing against the opposite side of my leg, trying to break through the skin. Ain't I supposed to have bones that prevent that kinda shit? Fingers penetrating legs and sadistic shit like that? One would think. So yeah. Obviously I start screaming and trying to get away, but his friends hold me down and tell me if I move, I'm gonna have holes in more places than just my leg. I try to stay still but holy fuck. Shit's about impossible in a moment like that. The pain was so intense I was praying to just pass out. Anything to get my mind off what he was doing. And he's still standing there, like almost a full minute later, although shit, who the fuck can really say in a moment like that, to be truthful it felt more like a year, not no minute, but hell, it could have been ten seconds for all I fuckin' know, him with his goddamn finger inside my leg, like he's searching for something he ain't ever gonna find. Taking the goddamn scenic route through my insides all willy-nilly-like."

"I'm gonna be sick." Ted tried to stand up, but the basement kept spinning, so he closed his eyes and banged the back of his skull against the deep freezer. "Please stop describing what he did."

Justin laughed. "You're acting as if you were the one who had to go through that shit. Nah, brother, he did it to me. And look, I'm still alive. I'm still standing. Well, still *sitting*, at least. And I'll probably only be alive for another couple hours. But still. I survived that motherfucker. I'm right here, brother. Right fucking here. Look. *Look.*"

SEVENTEEN

TED OPENED HIS EYES. SINCE HE'D CLOSED THEM, Justin had turned around and bent over the mattress and pulled down his pants, revealing his bare, hairy ass. Before Ted could respond to the hideous sight before him, Justin released a loud, disturbing fart.

"Oh, what the fuck." Ted scrambled to his feet and fled the room. Justin's laughter echoed through the basement. He sounded like a coked-up Joker. "You're such an asshole, man." Ted kept his distance, leaning against the torn couch in the basement's living room section. "Jesus Christ. What is wrong with you?"

Justin attempted to apologize in between hiccups of laughter, but all he managed to produce was a series of unintelligible squeaks. "More beer! We need more beer!"

"We drank it all."

"Fuck you. We need more beer!"

Ted sighed and went into the bathroom to take a shit. He sat on the toilet and dug out his phone. When had he put it back in his pocket? No clue. The battery was nearly dead anyway but that didn't stop him from casting another wave of texts Shelly's direction. He asked her if she was okay. He told her he loved her. He said he wanted to spend the rest of his life with her. Then he wiped his ass and flushed the toilet.

He remained seated afterward and stared at the closed door and wondered how long he could stay locked inside this room with a giant dog rampaging on the other side. Streaks of dried blood stained the floor. Or maybe it was feces. Who could tell? Ted wasn't an expert on either substance by any means. The humidity was worse in the bathroom than Justin's prison cell of a bedroom. When he rose, his ass cheeks briefly stuck to the toilet seat. Like velcro peeling apart, sound effect and all. He winced and washed his hands, avoiding his reflection in the mirror. He didn't want to see the face that Shelly no longer loved. One glimpse could destroy him. A thumbtack through a balloon.

Outside the bathroom, he considered which direction to take. Left returned him to Justin's room. Right led him upstairs, either out the back door or into the kitchen. Neither choice seemed very appealing. What would happen if he just stood still in front of the bathroom? Stood and closed his eyes and melted out of existence. Just stopped thinking. Nothing would happen. Justin would freak out and scream, thinking Ted had abandoned him. Midnight would come around. He'd still be chained to that ridiculous goddamn anchor. Ted's feet would eventually hurt. His legs would start shaking. Nothing remained stagnant. Everything always sank if you gave it enough time.

If Ted left Justin's house, he would drive directly to his mother-in-law's. What happened afterward frightened him more than anything that could ever happen in this basement. This basement was flooded with fiction. Facing Shelly would be the harshest goddamn reality he'd ever confronted.

Ted turned right. Stopped. Bit his lip. Dug his nails into

his palms. Whispered a word that'd shock a nun. Then he turned around and returned to the bedroom. Justin lay on the mattress in the fetal position, eyes closed, breathing heavily.

"Are you seriously asleep right now?"

Justin bolted up. His eyes widened and bounced around the room in a fit of delirium. "What? No. I'm awake. What's up?"

"You fucking fell asleep, didn't you?"

"No, I—"

Ted cut him off with his hand and slid back down the deep freezer onto the floor. "It's okay to sleep, man. It's not like you don't need it. Jesus, you look like you haven't slept in a year. Hell, *I* feel like I haven't slept in a year, so I can't even imagine what you're going through right now."

Justin rubbed his eyes. "Brother, that's the first sensible thing you've said all day. Shit, how long was I out? What time is it?"

"Only a couple minutes. Fifteen, max." Ted slipped his phone from his pocket and glanced at the time, then stared a second longer to ascertain his inbox hadn't received any new messages. "It's almost nine. You got three hours until midnight. Then I'm unlocking you and you're getting in my car and we're driving to the emergency room. I don't care if I have to drag your ass. You're going."

"Time's just zipping by, isn't it?"

"If you say so." Time certainly was not zipping by for Ted. Time was moving like a slasher victim through a forest. Everlasting, no end in sight, the threat of decapitation present the moment one dared to turn around. "Why midnight, anyway?"

"What?"

"Full moon's gonna be out way before midnight. Come

to think about it, it's probably already visible. How come you haven't wolfed out yet?"

Justin pointed straight up. "Werewolves don't transform until the moon is at the highest point in the sky. Tonight, that time is estimated to be around midnight."

"And how do you know this?"

Justin tossed up his arms like he was talking to a child. "From experience, bitch. What you think? Haven't you been listening to a word I've done told you? Also, the internet."

"Well, you didn't say that. I'm not the one who's a werewolf expert, now am I?"

"You know." Justin smirked and wiped saliva from his chin. "If you're interested, I can give you another sneak preview of that full moon."

"Show me your ass again and I'm going home."

Justin tsked. "Again with the homophobia."

"How is that homophobia? Name one person who would possibly want to look at your gross, disgusting ass."

"What's your mom up to these days?"

"Probably still fucking my dad."

"Yeah. Sounds like her, all right." He scratched his balls and cracked his neck. "Where was I, anyway?"

"In the story?"

"Where else?"

"Someone was digging his fingers into your leg."

Justin grimaced. "Ugh. Don't remind me."

"Then maybe don't forget your place in your own story."

"Then don't freak out whenever you see a little bit of ass."

"You're correct. That's my bad. My sincere apologies."

Justin nodded. "That's more like it. Now, yes, as I was saying. Donny, he's working me over, not saying anything. The act's so natural you'd think this is how he greets everybody."

"How are you so sure he doesn't?"

"You're right, Teddy. I'm not sure. He might." Justin wiped his nose and looked at whatever smeared across his hand. His brow arched. "So, after a while, Donny finally takes his finger out of my leg and sits back down as if he just shook my hand, all *formal* and shit. And he says, 'Now, I have a question. You say this event occurred last week, yet the fight was scheduled for *last night*. Why, pray tell, did you not ring somebody to inform them of this unfortunate turn of events? If you have a job, and you are sick to work, do you not call in and let your boss know so they can find somebody else to cover your shift? No. *Of course* you call. The world would be chaos if employees suddenly forgot how to use the telephone.'"

Ted licked his lips, choosing his reply carefully. "I mean. He *did* have a point…right?"

"Of course he had a fucking point. But, so what? Dude just probed my leg with his dirty-ass finger. Now you're on his side? What the hell?"

"No, I'm just saying, you could have called in. Probably prevented these guys from even coming to your house."

Justin sighed, looking at Ted like he couldn't believe what he was seeing. "You're a real asshole, you know that, Teddy?"

"What did I do?"

"No shit calling in would have prevented them from coming. Does it look like I got a fuckin' time machine to you?"

"You have a ship anchor. You could have anything. I don't know."

Justin eyed the anchor, then turned back to Ted. "You are a ridiculous specimen of humanity. Please stop talking."

"Ouch."

"Yes, he had a point. No, that didn't change the fact that I hadn't called. I was sick and out of my mind with a fever that whole week. And that's what I told Donny. I says, 'Look, man, I'm sorry, I wasn't thinking about anything besides not dying. I don't even know where my cell phone is right now. I completely forgot about the fight, and I'm truly sorry.' Sounds sincere, right?"

"I'd say so."

"Yeah, I thought so, too."

"But did Donny?"

"Fuuuuuck no."

"What happened?"

"First he says, 'Any normal fight, and sure, I'd be upset, but I'd also understand. Things happen. Sure. I get that.' But then he pauses for, like, dramatic effect or some shit, and continues with, '*However*, Saturday-night fights, particularly the *last* fight on a Saturday night, are anything but normal fights. They're what we call *main events*. And main events, dear Justin, are not cheap. People sometimes fly in from *out of state* to view these fights. Main events are reserved for the best of the best. Not just anybody can fight in a main event,' he says. 'Dogmen, they're required to pay a substantial participation fee. Think of it as a deposit you'd put down on an apartment. Only, if your dog dies at the end of your lease, you don't get any of it back.'"

"But...you didn't pay the fee, did you?" Ted scratched his head, trying to make sense of the situation.

"Man, I didn't even know there *was* a fee. No-Dick never said shit about it. And that's what I told Donny. I asked him what the hell he was talking about. Said nobody told me nothing about no fee. And Donny says, 'When I scheduled your fight, Ricky informed me you couldn't afford the deposit, yet he begged me to take you on. I suggested we start you off with something of less importance first, perhaps a Friday morning brawl, but Ricky persisted. He stated the dog you had would be wasted on something so small. He said it needed to be a main event. Begged me to excuse the fee, just this once. He said the kind of the dog you had was guaranteed to win, that it was a veteran fighter. So I think to myself, all right. Justin seems like a good kid. If he says he has a killing machine, maybe he does. So, out of good faith, I tell Ricky he has my approval, that I'll put up the deposit myself.'"

Ted felt like he was going to vomit again. "Oh no."

Justin nodded. They were finally on the same page. "Oh *yes,* brother. No-Dick convinced the fucking *leader* of the Hammond Dogfighting Association—or *whatever* the fuck you'd call it, *I* don't know—to pay my entry fee. I don't know how, but he fuckin' did it. And then I didn't show up! Which means Donny, he had to forfeit that entire fee to the dogman who *did* show up."

"How much was the entry fee?"

Justin burst out laughing. "That's exactly what I asked him! And do you know what he said?"

"I…do not."

"He says, 'Never you mind. I'm not interested in whatever pathetic amount of cash you have saved up in your little piggy bank.'"

"Then…what did he want?"

"I asked him that question, as well. And he told me… all he wanted was an apology. An apology for wasting not only his money, but also his time."

"An apology?"

"Yup."

"Well, that's not so bad."

Justin raised his index finger, excited. "One would think! And one would also be very, very wrong."

"Did you apologize?"

"First of all, I'd already apologized, if you recall. But yeah. I apologized again. I told him I was super sorry. Events happened I hadn't expected and I take full responsibility for being too stupid to call and cancel. He sits there at the table, listening to me, taking it in, and finally says, 'The thing about apologies is, anybody can give one away. They're so often meaningless. All a person has to do is open and close their mouth a few times.' And I'm sitting across from him, all tense, thinking oh shit, this don't sound too good, and by that point, if you're keeping track, I already got my werewolf senses."

"How could I forget?"

"So yeah. The senses were accurate. Shit was not good at all. Donny tells me, 'I'm going to need an apology from the heart. When you tell me you're sorry, I want to believe you really mean it. And let's be honest, it's never going to sound sincere here in your kitchen.' So I asked him where he'd like to hear it, and he nods behind me, toward the staircase, and says, 'Why don't we go for a little ride?' And this is the point where that whole fight or flight instinct everybody's always talking about kicked in, and my body punched in on flight hard enough to break the button. I jumped up from my chair and fucking hightailed it through the kitchen, forgetting all about how much my leg hurt. There was no way I'd make it down the stairs without his goons catching me—they were *right fucking there*—but I figured maybe I had a chance with the front door. I get past Donny and make it, like, five feet through the living room at the most when suddenly I'm on the ground, convulsing, this wave of *heat* tickling up and down my body."

"Heat?"

"Motherfuckers shot me with a taser." Justin flopped down on the mattress and mimicked a seizure.

"Oh."

He composed himself and sat back up. "Anyway, then one of them pulled a bag over my face and tied my hands behind my back with, like, this plastic shit, and led me downstairs and out the back door. I started protesting, you know, screaming for help, but it was useless. They threw me in a trunk and slammed it shut and drove off. And, yeah, that's when shit got really interesting."

EIGHTEEN

"I DON'T KNOW HOW LONG WE DROVE AROUND. IT FELT like the car would never stop. At one point, I may have fallen asleep, I'm not sure."

Ted cocked his head, both amused and terrified all at once. "You get kidnapped, and the first thing you do is fall asleep. Amazing."

"Bitch, you weren't there. You try riding around in a trunk for, like, an hour, see if you stay awake the whole time. Shit was suffocating. The lack of oxygen squeezed my brain like a sponge. I don't know if I officially fell asleep, okay, but I definitely got myself lost."

"Lost?"

"Yeah, lost. Lost in the darkness of it all. Not only was I in the trunk, but I still had that goddamn bag over my head. It was physically exhausting just trying to breathe with that fucking thing on. It was so dark I couldn't stand it. So I got lost. It wasn't intentional. All of my thoughts grew distant and took up shelter someplace far away. Muffled, like they were under water. I couldn't think. I felt like I was somewhere outside of my own body, like I'd drifted."

"Astral projection."

"What?"

"That's what you call it. When you leave your body like that. Astral projection."

"Well, that sounds like some goofy-ass nerd shit, man. I'm just telling you how it felt. You define it however the hell you want. All I'm saying is, time shifted and moved differently inside that trunk. I felt myself age and become an old man and gain wisdom no man has ever grasped. Of course, by the time the car finally stopped and the trunk opened, I'd forgotten all that wisdom, but it left a footprint. Something was there. Maybe it still is, only now it's just out of reach, teasing me."

Ted didn't know what the hell Justin was talking about. "The trunk opens and then what?"

Justin didn't skip a beat. "The bag's pulled off my face and I'm expecting to get nailed with a blast of sunlight, but somehow it's night already, and I'm looking up at two dark shadows. Both too fat and tall to be Donny. They reach in and drag me out and throw me on the ground. We're in this grass field and the wind is blowing strong enough to screw with my hearing, so it takes a moment for me to realize one of the guys is telling me to get up. Have you ever tried to stand with your hands tied behind your back? Shit ain't the easiest, let me tell you."

"No. I can't say that I have."

"I tried, but I kept falling back down. One of them got impatient and kicked me. Then the other one bent down and helped me up. So we're standing there in this field, and I'm thinking oh shit, they're about to put a bullet in my skull. The one who kicked me points at this barn a little ways in the field and says to walk, so I walk, not like I got much of a choice at this point. Look what happened last time I tried to run away, and I'd had control of both my arms then. Now? Not a fucking chance. We walk toward the barn, both of them behind me, and we're surrounded by the sound of crickets screwing. I start thinking of it as my death song, all these bugs shooting their tiny loads. Somehow it's soothing. I don't know why. It just is."

"Maybe you should pioneer the insect porn genre."

Justin considered the idea. "I would watch two crickets fuck. I don't know if I'd jerk off to it, but I'd definitely watch it."

"I can't think of anybody who wouldn't."

"Teddy, if I get out of this alive, you and me's teaming up and starting a production company. You might have something here."

"It would be an honor to film bugs having sex with you."

Justin grimaced. "What? I ain't fuckin' no bugs, dude."

"*What?* Why would you…?"

"You just said you'd film them having sex with me."

"No. I mean, I'd join you in—"

"You want to *join* me? What the fuck?"

"Never mind. Holy shit." Ted climbed up the deep freezer and leaned against it until the initial wave of light-headedness passed. "I gotta piss."

"You want me to watch, you sick piece of shit?"

Ted went and did his business. He washed his hands and forgot about avoiding his reflection until he was face-to-face with his own ugly mug. It took him a spell to recognize what was falling down his cheeks were tears. After he composed himself, he stepped outside on the back porch and made a phone call. It rang awhile, and when nobody answered it transferred him to its voicemail and told him to leave a message at the beep.

"Hey. It's me. Same as the last two thousand messages.

Just wanted you to know I was thinking about you, is all. I feel awful for bugging you so much. I know I'm not respecting your wishes and leaving you alone, but goddammit, baby, you have no idea how hard this is. Or maybe you do. I don't know. I'm just hurting, you know? I'm hurting so goddamn much I could die."

He hung up and went back into the basement. That was it. He wouldn't call her again. If she wanted to speak to him, then she could call for once. He was done begging.

NINETEEN

TED PACED BACK AND FORTH IN THE BEDROOM AS he spoke. Justin watched him moving with intrigue. "Let me guess. There was a full moon that night, right? The night the dogfighting people—the…the *dogmen*—abducted you."

Justin nodded, proud. "Indeed it was."

"So what happened? You wolfed out and made your escape or what?"

"Well, yeah. But it wasn't that simple."

"It sounds like it."

"Let me finish the story, then."

"I'm listening. Talk." Ted walked faster around the room. Memories of Shelly threatened to overflow his system. His head throbbed. He craved a distraction. "When did you transform?"

"Not until later." Justin opened his mouth to continue and fell into a coughing fit. When he was finished, a string of thick blood hung from his bottom lip. A few seconds passed and it dropped in his lap. He didn't seem to notice. "As soon as we push open the barn doors, a dozen or so dogs begin barking like crazy. One of the guys behind me pushes me forward and I nearly trip again, but manage to keep my balance. The barn smells much how you'd expect a barn full of angry fighter dogs to smell. Like shit. I look around and there are dogs locked up in cages on either side of me. Like a horse stable, is what it kinda reminds me of, you know? And at the end of the barn, there's Donny standing. Waiting for me. The first thing that crosses my mind is, did they really wait for him to get out of the car and walk into the barn and find a good, intimidating place to stand before opening the trunk and letting me out? Obviously I don't ask him that, but holy shit, it was all I could think about. Why not just have us all go together? It was killing me. But then I saw the sawed-off shotgun in Donny's hands, pointed straight at me."

"Shit."

"I stopped and tried talking to one of the guys behind me—you know, to, like, plead my case or whatever—but they wouldn't let me get more than a word in before pushing me again and telling me to move my ass. Meanwhile, Donny waited at the end of the barn, patient as can be, shotgun in his hands like it was a bouquet of flowers and I was his prom date and he couldn't wait to fuck. When I finally get up close to him he gestures the shotgun at an opened cell. It's empty, as far as I can see, which I take to believe means he wants me to fill its vacancy. But I just stand there and wait for further instructions. Truthfully, I'm so goddamn scared I'm not even sure if my legs will still listen to what I tell them to do at this point. Someone steps behind me and cuts off the plastic handcuffs from my wrists and Donny goes, 'Get in the cage or lose a limb. Your choice.' And maybe my legs won't listen to what I say but they sure as hell listen to what Donny's got to say, because they immediately move my ass inside that cage. Cage is a good word for it, too. He closes the gate behind me and claustrophobia hits as soon as the lock snaps in place."

"How big is it?"

"Standing, my head rubs against the ceiling, and if I extend both my arms out side to side, my fingertips touch each wall. So. Not very big."

Ted felt claustrophobic just thinking about it. The basement bedroom seemed a lot smaller than it had a few minutes ago. Were the walls slowly closing in? Was the house shrinking as they talked? It all sounded plausible. He was losing his mind, wasn't he? *Losing?* No. At this point his mind had been lost a long while, and he'd given up all hope of ever finding it again. It'd never done him a bit of good, anyway. Goodbye and don't come back, as far as he was concerned. Sayo-fuckin'-nara.

Hesitation stuttered Justin's speech as he continued. "The gates on each of the cages had a doggy door at the bottom. I noticed the one on the cell I was in almost immediately because it seemed like my only way out. It was either escape through there or sit and wait for whatever the fuck good ol' destiny had in store for me this time. I fell down on my hands and knees and tried crawling through it, head first, but it was locked from the outside, just like the rest of the gate. I may have started screaming some dirty words right about then, if memory serves me correctly."

"I wouldn't blame you if you had." Ted could imagine a few words he'd yell if thrown into a similar situation. None of them could exactly be defined as "clean" by even the thinnest of definitions.

"Shall I repeat those words?" Justin leaned forward with a grin on his face, like they were just boys again and his mom was upstairs fixing supper, oblivious to the new vocabulary they'd recently acquired at school from the older kids who smoked in the bathroom during lunch.

"I don't think that's necessary." Although a small part of Ted did want Justin to say the words.

Justin shrugged, bounced out of his childlike trance. "At least they were kind enough not to let the mystery of what they had planned linger for too long. A couple minutes after I stopped trying to pry open the doggy door, Donny unlocked it. Except before I could even consider escaping, a big-ass fuckin' pit pull stuck its snout through and glared at me. Donny had the same kinda expression on his face as the dog, only through the top of the gate instead of the bottom. He says, 'You wanted to fight dogs, so you fight dogs. And if you win, maybe then you can apologize for your carelessness.'"

"Oh. Oh no."

"Yeah. 'Oh no' about sums it up, don't it? I start to scream something, I don't remember what now, probably to beg him to please change his mind, if I had to guess, but he cuts me off by shouting some German word, I don't know what exactly, but I recognized it as something a lot of dogmen say when a fight starts, and before I can utter another word the pit bull's growling and gunning toward me. I have exactly one second to think before the fucking thing's tackling me to the ground, its teeth digging into my forearm." He held up his right arm for emphasis.

"I don't see any marks."

"Another thing I've learned. Werewolves tend to heal pretty fast."

"What about your leg then?"

"I think it's different when it comes to the bite that turns you."

"You read that on the internet, too?"

"No, but I don't see any other way of explaining it. Do you?"

"So the dog's biting you…then what?"

"Well, it kept on fucking biting me, that's what. I thought it was going to tear my arm clean off. I was on my back and it was on top of me, face inches away from my face, my arm the only thing preventing it from tongue-kissing me. My blood started spilling down into my eyes and I couldn't see a goddamn thing, could just feel this agonizing pain and hear its growling and snarling increase in its insanity as it gnawed away on my flesh, *on my fucking bone*, and I know if I don't do something right now, I'm fucked, it's over, I'm done for. If I can just roll over and press all of my weight on top of the dog, maybe I'll have a chance. Once I'm on top of it, I don't know, I guess I try to strangle it or gouge my thumbs through its eyes. As long as I don't let its goddamn mouth near my throat, I'll be fine. But that's all fairy tale thinking because try as hard as I can, I cannot roll the fuck over, and this dog is only getting closer to my neck, closer to my throat. Then I hear someone shout something, I don't know, maybe another German command, I'm so out of it I wouldn't have understood basic English, and the dog immediately releases my arm and runs back out of the doggy door, leaving me on the ground covered in blood, shaking and crying and coming to terms with the fact that I've gone and pissed my pants. But so what. You're allowed to piss your pants when a dog's fuckin' killing you."

"I believe I've heard that rule before," Ted joked, but in reality he felt like he'd nearly wetted himself as well, just from listening to the story. Nausea held him in its grip and it refused to relent.

"I might have even shit a little, too, if I'm being completely honest."

"Also acceptable, given the circumstances. Although, maybe a little too much information?"

Justin lowered his face toward his lap, ashamed. "I also came."

"You also...*came*?"

Justin nodded, like what he was saying wasn't unreasonable or crazy in the slightest. "Yup. Jizzed all over the place."

"What the fuck."

"What?"

"Why would...why would you do that?"

"I don't know. It's a werewolf thing, I guess."

"Jesus fucking Christ."

Justin laughed hard enough to shoot out snot. "Nah, man, I'm just screwing with you."

"Oh."

"But I did shit myself, though."

"Okay."

"And pee."

"It's okay."

"Imagine if I *had* come, though. Oh, man. How weird would that have been?"

"Pretty weird."

Justin was quiet. Shame settled in between them. "So, uh...anyway, they have the dog come back out of my cage and they lock the doggy door and Donny's still standing there at the gate, watching me, this smug-ass smile on his face as he looks down at me on the ground, all bloody and crying and just a big goddamn mess, and he says, 'Now I want you to apologize. Like you really mean it.' And I do. I scream that I'm sorry, I scream it over and over again, blood and snot spilling in my mouth and making me choke, yet I don't stop screaming it. Finally, Donny tells me that's enough, and I manage to quiet down, and he says, 'I'm not completely convinced. We'll let you sit and think about your actions awhile, then you'll go another round with Maximus. See how you're feeling afterward.' And they leave the barn, get in their car, and drive away. I can hear the engine getting farther and farther. Maybe they're going to get something to eat, maybe they're going to bed, who the hell knows. My mind's racing a mile a second. I start screaming for somebody to help me, which only makes all the dogs in the barn start howling along with me, and I realize screaming isn't gonna do any good. There's a reason this barn is way out in the middle of nowhere, right? All isolated from curious ears. Screaming ain't gonna accomplish shit except make my throat sore. That becomes clear to me but does that actually stop me from doing it? Hell no. I just start screaming louder. Not even words anymore. Just these animal noises. Howls that match the pitch of the dogs. The dogs jailed up just like I'm jailed up. We're all prisoners here. We're begging for the same escape. All howling at that beautiful, full moon barely visible through the cracks in the top of the far wall in the barn."

Ted nodded and made an *ah-ha* face. "And now's when you wolf out."

Justin bobbed his head with him. "Yes. Now's when I wolf out. I think."

"You think?"

"Well, my memory ain't the best, but here's what I definitely remember: I was on the floor, I was screaming, or howling, or whatever, and I kept looking at the moon through the cracks in the wall, then it felt like someone or some*thing* was ripping the skin off my bones, and this intense pain shot through my body, so powerful it about paralyzed me, and then…I blacked out."

"You blacked out."

"Yeah. Like I was drunk. No memory of what happened next whatsoever. One minute I'm on the floor, crying, then I'm waking up the next day sprawled out in the field under the sun, nude as the day I was pried from my momma's womb, covered head to toe in blood."

"Yours?"

Justin shook his head, fear in his eyes.

"Then whose?"

"My head was pounding. My body felt like it was on fire, which made sense, because it had to have been almost noon and the sun was in a fierce mood. If I stayed there in the field, my skin would surely melt off. It might have already if not for the layers of blood protecting my nudity, which I understand sounds like a fucked-up way to think, but that's the way it was, so if you want to say something, maybe just keep it to yourself."

"I wasn't going to say anything."

"You had that look in your eyes."

"What look?"

"That 'Wow, Justin, you sure are talking like a psychopath' look."

"I…I don't know what you're talking about." Of course Ted knew what he was talking about, but hell, wasn't like he could admit such a thing, now could he?

"Mmm-hmm." Justin cracked his knuckles and yawned. Already tired with his own story. The night continued getting later. Sooner or later it'd be showtime. Shit or get off the pot. "I could see the barn from where I stood, but it wasn't exactly close. I didn't even know where I was, considering they'd not only had a bag over my head, but I'd also been in the trunk during the whole car trip. It took a good half hour or so to walk back to the barn, and the whole time I'm telling myself how stupid I am, that I'm clearly walking right into a death trap. Donny's probably inside right now, scratching his head and wondering how I managed to escape, and it's not like I can explain how, either. I passed out and woke up in a field. That's all I know. And somehow I got covered in blood, which I mean, yeah, is pretty unsettling the more I think about it, so I stop thinking about it and just walk. If it's a death trap, then fuck it, maybe this is what I deserve. I know I sure as hell just can't keep wandering the field in my current state. If Donny doesn't find me, some other asshole will probably shoot me down the moment they lay eyes on me. I mean. I look like a goddamn zombie, let's be honest. I'd probably shoot me, too."

"Instead you want me to." Ted didn't have to look down at the revolver to know it was still on the ground next to him. The heat of its steel radiated off his leg. Imagined or not, he could *feel* it.

"Yes. That's correct. And also rude. Didn't that hot mother of yours ever teach you not to interrupt?"

"Sorry."

"First thing I notice is Donny's car parked in front of the barn. The passenger door is wide open and the interior overhead light is on. Dim, but on. The windshield's smashed, too, and blood stains the tips of the surrounding shards. There's also an alarming amount of blood inside the car, soaked into both the front and back seats. But just blood, no…bodies. The bodies I find inside the barn, along with a mountain of dog corpses. All of them torn inside out and gutted. I don't mean just the dogs. The…*bodies*. The human bodies. Donny and two of his friends. I can barely recognize them. The sight, the smell, all of it, it's too much. I run to the corner of the barn and vomit, and as the puke's coming out of me, I realize I'm making a mess all over Donny's head. It's—it's been…*ripped* off his body. Just…fucking…*decapitated*."

TWENTY

Ted had never met Donny, but that didn't prevent him from picturing the man's severed head, with perfect clarity, covered in Justin's vomit. By the queasy look on Justin's face, the real memory was one-hundred-percent worse than what Ted imagined. But was the memory real?

That was the question, right? If the severed head story was real, then how did the head get severed? Justin was fucking crazy, no doubt about it, but was he decapitate-a-person crazy? Ted didn't think so. At least, he didn't *want* to think so. They'd grown up together. They'd been best friends, for Christ's sake. A kid should know if his best friend's capable of growing up into someone who's going to eventually rip the head off another man.

So what did that mean, then? That Justin really was some—what? Some fucking…*werewolf*? Werewolves weren't real. Ted refused to allow that theory to play. Once he started letting werewolves in, then draculas and frankensteins would follow, along with the last few ounces of his remaining sanity.

Ted looked at his reflection in the bathroom mirror and imagined his mouth opening, imagined a thick stream of vomit spraying against the glass and ricocheting back into his face. It seemed like he thought about bodily fluids more and more as the night progressed.

Where did that leave Justin, then? He wasn't a werewolf, but that didn't mean he wasn't something else of equal terror. He believed Justin had purchased a fighter dog off of a stranger on Craigslist, and he believed that dog had bitten him on the leg. One look at Justin's calf and even a blind man wouldn't dare deny it. Maybe the dog *had* been diseased as Justin theorized, but not with some werewolf curse. The dog could've been rabies-stricken. It seemed plausible that a human infected with rabies would be liable to commit acts of extreme violence. Ted wasn't an expert by any stretch, but he failed to see any other explanation. Unless Justin had made up everything that had happened in the barn. But the look on his face was sincere. Sincere and frightened. Ted believed him. Believed him as best as he could.

When Ted sat back down against the deep freezer, Justin rubbed his stomach and groaned. "Feel like making another McDonald's run, brother?"

"You cannot be hungry. Not after telling the story you just told."

"The stomach wants what the stomach wants."

"I'm not going back to McDonald's."

"Fine." He huffed and puffed like a child throwing a tantrum. "It's probably a wise idea. Wouldn't want you getting a flat tire and leaving me here to transform all on my lonesome."

"Right."

"What time is it, anyhow?"

"A little past ten."

Justin clapped his hands and rubbed them together, up and down, excited. "Hot damn! It's nearly time, ain't it?"

"You seem awfully happy for a guy who's supposedly about to get shot."

"It's what comes after the shot that I'm looking forward to the most."

"And what's that?"

"Nothing."

"Nothing?"

"Sweet, beautiful nothing. Oh, Teddy, don't it sound glorious?"

"Sure."

In a way, it *did* sound glorious. He even kind of envied Justin—not that he was really going to shoot him, but still. It wouldn't be so bad, would it? Maybe there was a reason Justin had loaded the revolver with two bullets instead of one.

"All right, so you wake up in the field, you're naked, the barn's a bloodbath. What do you do next?"

"Well, do you remember how I said running wildly through the field would be a terrible idea?" He sighed, long and heavy. "I'm still amazed nobody shot me."

"You ran home naked?"

"Not home, no. Remember, at this point, I still have no idea where I am. I can't even begin to process what the hell I just discovered inside the barn. The more I think about it, the worse my head hurts. I pick a direction and start running. Naked. Bloody. A true maniac. Definitely not the best sight for a stranger to stumble upon. But I figured if I at least ran, then nobody would mistake me for a zombie."

"Why's that?"

Justin looked at him like he was stupid. "Because zombies don't run…?"

Now Ted gave him the same look in return. "First of all, zombies are fictional, and—"

"—Fictional like *werewolves?*—"

"—*and secondly*, zombies totally can too run."

"What? No, they can't."

"They did in *28 Days Later.*"

Justin sneered. "Those weren't real zombies."

"Then what were they?"

"I don't know. But zombies can't run. They shamble. That right there is a fact."

"Didn't you make fun of me earlier for suggesting zombies were real?"

"Teddy, buddy, I will make fun of you for any reason at any time. It don't matter if it contradicts my own beliefs. Your shame is what's most important here."

"Oh. Okay. Yeah, that makes sense."

"I'm glad you're starting to come around. I'm real proud of ya."

Ted laughed and shook his head. "You're such an asshole."

"Thank you."

"What about the *Dawn of the Dead* remake?"

"Teddy, you will not speak blasphemy in my house."

"What? That movie was great."

"Remakes are sacrilegious, and I will not tolerate their presence."

"That's crazy."

"Then I don't want to be sane."

"What about *The Thing*?"

Justin scrunched up his face. "What thing?"

"You know. The movie. *The Thing.*"

"What about it?"

"I thought that was, like, your favorite movie."

"Yeah? So what?"

Ted had him now. "Well, that's a remake."

"Fuck you. *The Thing* ain't no remake."

"Uh-huh, is too." Ted readjusted his position on the floor, eager to break Justin's cynicism. "The original was made in the fifties or sixties, or something. A long time ago. I swear to God. It's a remake."

Justin rolled his eyes. "*The Thing* is adapted from some old-ass book. It was called something like *Halt! Who Goes There?* or some shit. So yes. You're correct. Before Carpenter got his hands on it, some other asshole tried adapting it. That doesn't make Carpenter's film a remake. The source material was always the *book*, not the other movie. So nice try, motherfucker."

"Oh." Ted struggled to conjure a comeback. Nothing came. "I didn't know that."

"Yeah, no shit."

"How did you get home, then?"

"What?"

"You're running naked through a field, covered in blood. How did you get home?"

"Oh." Justin nodded and leaned back against the ship anchor. "Well, first, I broke into the first house I came across and took a shower."

"Jesus Christ."

"Eh. It wasn't that dangerous. We're talking a Monday afternoon here, right? I figured there was a good chance nobody would even be home, and guess what? I was right. And plus, I didn't even really break in, if you want to get technical about it. Dumbasses left their back door un-locked. Nice house, too. All tidy and clean like somebody

actually cared about it. Yet they leave their back door unlocked. Good luck solving that mystery."

"Maybe they never thought someone would ever have
the guts to just open the door and walk in."

"Bullshit. I say if a person ain't always expecting to get
robbed and murdered, then that person is a fool and de-
serves whatever happens to them."

"That's some sound logic you got there."

"Truth be told, they're lucky it was me who came upon
their house and not some deranged lunatic."

"Well—"

"Teddy, shut the fuck up." Justin flipped him the bird,
just in case he didn't get the message. "But, no. The house
was empty. Before walking in, I stuck my head through the
door and did the whole, 'Hello! Is anybody home?' thing
people always do in movies. Nobody answered me, so I
figured it was fine to stroll on inside. I mean, if they didn't
want me in their house, then they would have said something, right?"

"Sure. That makes sense."

"First thing I did was, I took a shower. It was upstairs,
so sadly I did have to track muddy footprints all over the
place. Also got some blood on the walls. And a little bit
of semen from an unrelated incident. Trust me, it was un-
avoidable. The shower took longer than I expected, but
given how filthy I'd gotten, I'm surprised I managed to
scrub it all off of me. I thought bloodstains were supposed
to be a bit more permanent, like that blue dye stuff bank
tellers hide in wads of cash to bamboozle thieves."

"I have never been covered in blood nor have I robbed
a bank, so I can't really say."

"I'm just glad nobody was waiting for me outside the

bathroom once I finally finished. I was convinced that as soon as I opened the door, some lady would be standing there with a tiny pistol pointed directly in my face, relieved to finally have a chance to blow somebody's head off. But nope. House was still empty. I found some clothes in the closet and got dressed. A little baggy on me but that was okay."

"Not only did you break in and use their shower, but you also stole their clothes?"

"Would you have preferred I kept walking around naked, Teddy?"

"Fair point."

"I can get naked right now, if you want. I don't mind."

"I'm okay."

Justin sniggered. "So, I'm dressed in my new digs and I'm thinking I'm pretty fucking hungry, which I'm sure don't come as no surprise to you."

"I've never seen somebody eat so many cheeseburgers in one sitting."

"Get the *Guinness Book of World Records* on the line."

"I lost their number."

"Oh, great fuckin' job, Teddy. You've ruined everything."

"I'm sorry."

"So I mosey down to the kitchen to see what kinda grub they got to work with."

"If only they'd been home to tell you not to eat their food. How else would you have known they wouldn't have liked that."

"Exactly! Let me tell you something, Teddy, I hit the goddamn jackpot. In the fridge I found the leftovers of half a roast beef. Shit was delicious. After all this time, though, I swear I can still taste it. Just a little bit. But the thing was, even after all that roast was gone, I still felt like I was starving. I craved meat. I thought maybe I was suffering some kind of, uh—what do you call it?—*protein* deficiency. I don't know. It made sense at the time. What else could it have been, right? I search the fridge some more and all I really find that's worth a damn is a tube of raw hamburger meat. One look at it and my hunger went apeshit. I had the tube split open and the meat squeezing into my mouth before I even realized it was happening."

"That isn't disgusting at all."

"You wouldn't say that to a pregnant woman."

It took Ted a couple seconds to fully register what Justin had said. "Wh-what?"

"Aren't pregnant women supposed to get strange cravings? Like, paint chips and whatnot? Would you call a pregnant woman disgusting? I bet you would, you rude piece of shit."

"You're not pregnant."

"No, but I'm something else."

"Werewolves and pregnant women are nowhere near the same thing."

"They ain't *that* much different."

"Yes…they are."

"Agree to disagree, then." Justin shrugged. "So yeah. I licked that hamburger wrapper clean. Like the lids of those pudding cups we used to eat at school. Do they still make those? Goddamn, those were the best back in the day."

"I'm sure pudding still exists, yes."

"Are you sure? When was the last time you've seen some? Like, in person?"

"Today's not the day to start a pudding conspiracy."

"Today's the only day I got." He paused, looking at Ted like he expected an argumentative response. When he didn't receive one, he continued. "I also found two twenty-dollar bills on the kitchen table, which kind of freaked me out, to be honest. What kind of maniac leaves cash sitting around their house, just out in the open like that? I tell you this, nobody in my family and none of the families I grew up with would have ever dared leave something valuable where anybody can see. They kept their shit hidden and trusted not even their grandmas. Because you know what? Grandmas steal, too, Teddy. Grandmas steal, too."

"You took the money, didn't you?"

"Hell yeah, I took the money. What do I look like to you, some kind of school teacher?"

"You look like the opposite of a school teacher."

"Come to think about it, actually, teachers probably steal just as much as grandmas. Teachers don't make shit."

"Imagine a grandma who was also a teacher."

Justin sighed, content with whatever image he conjured. "The most badass outlaw to ever set foot on Earth."

"I'm sure there are lots of teachers out there who also happen to be grandmas."

"Yup. And those are the ones you absolutely do not want to fuck with." Justin coughed, and this time he didn't even pretend to cover his mouth. A drop of something red flew across the room and landed out of sight. "So yeah, I swiped the cash. I figured if they left it on a kitchen counter, then it wasn't like they were desperate, right? They weren't dependent on it, or whatever the fuck. Then I used their house phone and called a cab, gave them the address listed on the front porch."

"I'm amazed they had a house phone."

"Exactly. I mean, do they have cell phones, too? What's the point of both? When you think about it, they kind of deserved to get robbed. They're just wasteful, ignorant people."

"You've never even met these people." Ted laughed, then stopped. "Don't tell me they came home and busted you."

Justin shook his head, a peculiar smirk across his face like maybe he wished they had. "Nah, man. Nobody ever showed except the cab. Turned out I was way out in Joliet, by the way. Where that old prison is, the one that closed down."

Ted brightened with recognition. "The one they used in *The Blues Brothers,* right?"

"Fuckin' A, man. Goddammit, that movie was the shit. Same dude who made *An American Werewolf in London,* AKA *My Life Story*, only if it was set in America present day, and there weren't any hot nurses, and there was a ship anchor in the guy's basement. Okay, maybe not exactly the same thing, but still pretty dang close."

"Is it, though?"

"Well, we're both fuckin' werewolves, ain't we?"

"I don't know. We'll see, I guess."

Justin laughed and his eyes slightly watered. "You haven't believed a word I've said, even still. Unbelievable."

"I'm still listening. If I thought you were completely crazy, I would have left a long time ago." Which wasn't exactly true. Where else did Ted have to go? It was either here or his mother-in-law's house, and nothing good was waiting for him there.

Justin relaxed a little and rubbed his face. "I'm not done with my story, either, so prepare to keep right on listening. It'll be midnight soon enough, then you'll see for yourself, anyway. But until then…"

TWENTY-ONE

66 THE CAB DROPS ME OFF A BLOCK FROM MY HOUSE. For one thing, in case the police investigating the break-in back in Joliet tracked down my driver, I didn't want him snitching my address, and plus, I was pretty paranoid someone would be waiting inside my house. A friend of Donny's, I guess. One of his fuckboys wondering where the hell he was at. I paced in my back yard for a while, trying to build up the guts to go inside and face the music. I was convinced someone would be waiting to blow my brains out as soon as I walked through the door. But the house was empty. I searched every inch of this place and found nobody. I made sure the front door was still locked and slid an old shelf against the back door, since the lock was now destroyed. I tried to piece together in my head what the fuck had happened back at the barn, but no answer I came up with made a lick of sense. I mean, think about it, Teddy, put yourself in my shoes. You get abducted by these lunatics, locked up in a cell and tortured by a fightin' dog, pass out, then wake up the next day covered in the blood of those who nabbed you in the first place. Everybody's dead except you. Who killed them? Well, who else is left standing? Did you do it, even if you don't got

no memory of it? If so, fuckin' *how?* See what I mean? Shit just don't add up unless I'd been blessed with some kinda guardian angel, but if that was the case, why did she wait so long to step in? What the fuck, was she on a lunch break or something? It would have been helpful if she'd jumped in *before* that dog had nearly eaten my goddamn arm off."

Justin's expression evolved from amusement to a ghastly sincerity. He sat at the edge of the mattress and waited for some kind of explanation. Practically begged for one.

Ted bit his tongue but chickened out once the pain hit. "I don't think guardian angels are real."

Justin's cheeks reddened. "Yeah, well, you also still don't believe werewolves are real, either."

"I've never said that."

"What? Dude, you've said it like a thousand times tonight. You've said it more than any other human being in history."

"Well. Okay. But I haven't said it in at least an hour."

"Does that mean you believe me now?"

"I don't know what I believe."

"Regardless of what you *believe,* here's what I *know:* that day I came back to the house, I barricaded myself inside and hid in my closet all night with a case of beer and a steak knife. I was so goddamn afraid any second someone would come kicking down my door. My heart kept beating like it was about to explode. My concentration was shot. Every bit of me was consumed by worry. The night got darker and I got drunker. I passed out and when I woke up, I wasn't in the closet no more. Sunlight burned into my retinas and hot cement sizzled my ass cheeks. I was in the middle of some street. Naked. Covered in blood. Body aching. Stomach full. It had happened again, the same thing—the same kind of blackout—that I'd experienced back at the barn."

"Whose blood was it this time?" Nausea whirled in Ted's stomach. He wasn't sure if he asked the question because Justin wanted him to ask it or because Ted was legitimately interested. He didn't want to buy into this bullshit, but it was getting more difficult to determine what *was* bullshit and what wasn't.

"How the fuck should I know? I didn't even know how I'd gotten there, right? Nothing made sense. I ran back home, still naked. Somehow nobody seemed to notice me. Maybe I just lucked out and passed through town at the right time of day when everybody was either asleep or at work. I don't know. When I got home, I found the shelf I'd used to barricade the back door shattered, destroyed. The closet door was hanging half off its hinges and the wood was all clawed up, like if I'd locked a dog inside the closet or something, except there was no dog. It was just me. Inside the closet I found bits and pieces of clothing, all shredded and torn. It was what I'd been wearing when I fell asleep the previous night."

"What closet?"

"The one in the laundry room. What, you want to go check? You don't believe me?"

"Yeah. I want to see it." Ted fully expected Justin to come up with some excuse. Maybe he'd gotten it fixed since then or replaced it with a brand new door, which wouldn't explain why he hadn't also fixed the lock on the back door.

But Justin only nodded, like maybe he'd already anticipated this and planned ahead. "Yeah, okay. Good idea."

Ted hesitated, then stood and stumbled out of the bedroom, toward the laundry area across from the bathroom.

The floor was composed more of discarded clothing than cement. Ted stepped around forgotten underwear like they were ancient mines. One false step and *ka-blam*. In the corner of the room, next to the sink, the closet door hung loosely from its hinges, deformed and severely clawed. It'd gone ten rounds and barely survived to tell the tale. If Justin was delusional, he was at least dedicated, too.

But *was* he delusional?

Ted scratched his head and stared at the closet door and wondered just what the hell he was supposed to do in this kind of situation. They never mentioned any crazy shit like this back in school. Nobody prepared you for the possibility of your best friend transforming into a werewolf.

It occurred to him then that, outside of the movies, he might be the first person something like this had ever happened to. It was kind of cool, in a way. Kind of cool, but mostly terrifying. What the fuck was he going to do?

"Teddy! You get lost in there, buddy?"

Justin's voice sounded desperate. Afraid.

Ted returned to his spot next to the padlocked deep freezer. "You weren't kidding about that door."

"I wasn't kidding about a lot of other things, either."

"Uh-huh."

"After I saw that door, oh man, shit just started hitting me hard. That something really was wrong with me. I know, it should have been obvious a lot sooner. Call it denial. Call it me being a stupid son of a bitch. I was concerned more people were murdered in a hideous way, like Donny and his crew, so I turned on the news, but all that was on was fuckin' *Family Feud* so I turned it back off and searched the news websites on my phone. Sure enough, first thing I see—first thing I see *after* the latest dumbass bullshit

Trump's tweeted, of course—is that these two homeless dudes got themselves mutilated by what appeared to be some kind of wild animal. Some jogger discovered their bodies at the park. The one by the Burger King that used to be a Wendy's. The report speculated it was either done by a pack of rabid dogs or even a black bear. I guess one was spotted over in Michigan City a few years back. Fuckin' news to me. Did you know Indiana had bears?"

"First werewolves, now bears. Great."

"Sarcasm will not protect you against my mighty claws, Teddy."

"It might. You don't know."

"In any case. This was no goddamn bear that killed these hobos. I knew the truth. Maybe not the *whole* truth, but I got the general gist, all right. Their deaths were, somehow, my responsibility. The blood I'd washed off in the shower belonged to them. I'd killed them just as I'd killed Donny and his crew the day before. I knew I was different now, that my body was changing. There were too many signs. Did I think the word *werewolf* just yet? No. But I suspected something similar, yeah, you bet. I mean, shit. The past two nights the moon had been full and I blacked out both times, then woke up the next morning covered in blood and connected to brutal murders. Even my goddamn clothes had been ripped to pieces. How else do you explain that shit?"

Ted didn't know how to respond. He remained motionless on the floor, staring at the wall, too afraid to look Justin in the eyes. But he could feel Justin's eyes on him and it burned like radiation and he hated it.

"Tell me, Teddy. Try to use some imagination for once and put yourself in my place. What would you think, huh?

What would you *do?*"

Ted didn't even hesitate. "I'd turn myself into the police."

"Bullshit. And say what?"

"That I've been blacked out two nights in a row and woke up with someone else's blood on me and I suspect I may be involved in multiple murders."

"Yeah? And how do you reckon the cops are gonna help you come the next full moon? You're just gonna be responsible for more death. More bloodshed. Don't think I haven't thought about it. Early on, once everything started making sense about what I might be, jail seemed like the only viable option for a guy like me—a…a *thing* like me. Every night, locked away in a tiny cell with no chance of escape? Hell yeah. Sign me up. But then I got to thinking. What if I got myself stuck with a cellmate? I'd only end up tearing the poor man's heart out. Maybe he'd deserve it, maybe not, who's to say, right? I ain't no god. I got no right to judge who gets what. But let's say I don't get a roommate, and I'm all alone in a cell. You think if a guard notices in the middle of the night one of his prisoner's been replaced with a weird-ass wolf creature, he ain't gonna investigate? What if he's foolish enough to open the door? Carnage is creeping at the end of every path except the one you and me's on right now. It's the only way. I gotta die, Teddy, and you gotta help me do it."

TWENTY-TWO

TED CRACKED HIS KNUCKLES AND STRETCHED across the floor, flat on his back. "Something I don't understand."

Justin lay across the mattress, head rubbing against the ship anchor, sharing the same view as Ted, like they were kids looking up at the stars together. "What's that?"

"A full moon only happens once a month, I thought. How is it you're wolfing out on consecutive nights like this?"

Justin laughed. "The way you ask that question, it's like you're this…this *critic* pointing out some plot hole. Like this whole night's been written down and choreographed purely for your entertainment." He sat up and glared at him, fuming. "Bitch, this is my fucking *life* we're talking about. I don't know every detail. I barely know *any* details. No fuckin' wise werewolf mentor passed along some ancient scroll for me to take home and study. There ain't no goddamn lycanthrope prophecy for us to gush over. It's me by myself having to deal with some bullshit that, until recently, I thought was real only in movies. So, no. I got no fuckin' idea why I turn when I do. Shit, son, if you want to get *really* technical about it—a real, legit full moon lasts only about a second. Blink and you've miss it."

"Oh, yeah, that's true."

"I have never claimed to know shit about shit. All I know is what happens to me when the moon is big and bright and everybody's asleep. Actually, scratch that, because I don't *really* know what happens to me, now do I? I can just take a guess based off the evidence given to me upon waking up. And all evidence points to me being a weregoddamnmotherfucking*wolf*."

The longer Justin talked, the less insane he sounded. Ted wished like hell he'd just shut up—the both of them. Yet he continued to prod. He couldn't help himself. "I can't wrap my head around this."

Justin shrugged. "No one's asking you to."

"Just…the logistics of it all."

"Yeah, it's fuckin' weird, man. Trust me. I know."

"So, the dog you bought off Craigslist, its bite is what turned you into a…"

"Go on. Say the word."

"A werewolf."

Justin grinned. "Attaboy." He cracked his neck and stretched his legs out. "And yeah. Of course it was that fuckin' dog. Well, okay, it wasn't really a dog, but you know what I mean."

"So you think it was a werewolf, too."

"Nothing else would make much sense, now would it?"

Ted leaned forward, thoughts overheating. "But that would mean he was also a man, or a woman, I guess. When he wasn't…wolfed out. It was a human."

"Correct."

Ted held out both hands, confused. "So then, what the fuck was this guy doing in the cage, and why was that other guy selling him? How does that make any sense to you? It's crazy."

Justin paused. "I hadn't thought about that."

"Were they roommates who had a falling out? Was the Craigslist guy some werewolf hunter? So many possibilities, and all of them are stupid."

"Teddy. Promise me you won't sell me on Craigslist."

Ted cleared his throat, staring Justin in the eyes. "You know I can't promise that."

"Oh, you motherfucker."

Ted tried not to laugh but couldn't help it. He didn't want to laugh. Laughter felt like betrayal. "What happened the next night? Did you black out again, wake up in your birthday suit?"

Justin shook his head, face sunken with exhaustion. "Not that night, no. But let me tell you, that whole day I was fuckin' petrified. Took me ages to fall asleep. I kept pacing around my house, driving myself up the fuckin' wall, pulling my hair out of my skull. I didn't know what to do. I didn't know what was happening. I was just afraid of the night. So, so afraid. I tried calling No-Dick, but his phone would go straight to voicemail. In fact, I've been trying to call that bastard since what happened at the barn, and I've yet to hear shit."

"Do you think he…knows? About what's going on with you?"

Justin breathed in deep and heavy before responding. Reminded Ted of a TV doctor preparing to deliver terrible news. "What I think is, my house wasn't the first place Donny and his boys stopped at. After all, I wasn't the one who called Donny up and begged him to take the bet, right? That was all No-Dick. Seems to me like his house would've been the first place Donny hit."

"You think Rick's dead?"

"I think there's probably a good reason he hasn't been answering his phone."

Ted rubbed his jaw. He hadn't done this much talking in years and he was beginning to feel the side-effects. "So is that it? Anything else you gotta tell me?"

Justin laughed. His throat sounded raspy and worn out. "Anything else? Dude. I just spilled my fuckin' guts out, and you're asking what else, like what I said wasn't enough, like it wasn't no big thing. Teddy, man, I've fuckin' killed people. What the fuck?"

"I'm sorry. I don't mean it like that. Calm down." Ted leaned against the deep freezer and immediately sat forward, afraid he'd fall asleep if he got too comfortable. "What I was saying was, did anything else happen after that? You know. How long ago did this even happen? Surely there's been other full moons, right?"

"Oh, there's been plenty."

"And…?"

He licked his lips. "You ain't a priest and I ain't about to confess every one of my sins. Some things I'm keeping to myself."

"Things worse than what you've already told me?"

He nodded, sadness in his eyes. "I'll tell you one more thing. Then you're gonna need to answer some questions of my own."

"Uh. Okay."

Justin stared off into nothingness for a spell before clearing his throat and redirecting his attention back to Ted. "So, all right, after those first two incidents, you gotta understand my state of mind. I basically fell into this pit of constant fear. Paranoia became my best friend, and it tagged along wherever I went. I was convinced the police would come knocking on my door, that I'd left behind all this evidence during…whatever it was I'd actually done. I still don't know, but back then? I was like a blind kid lost in…in some strange city. I was stumbling and reaching out for anything to guide me. I hadn't associated the blackouts with the moon yet. As far as I knew, it could hit me any time of any day. I refused to leave the house for almost a month. Of course, I eventually had to go out for food. Despite how freaked out I was, my stomach remained this endless abyss of hunger. I couldn't stop thinking about the goddamn meat I'd stolen from that house in Joliet. It was more than just a craving. It was like…like okay, imagine you're swimming, right, and you're at the bottom of a real deep pool and for some idiotic reason you open your mouth—suddenly your body's going into shock and demanding you give it oxygen immediately, or *else*. That's how my hunger felt."

"Sounds like you had a tapeworm."

"I think you mean a *were*worm."

"What?"

Justin shrugged. "It sounded better in my head."

"Obviously."

"So, I made myself get off my lazy ass and drive to the grocery store. I grabbed a shopping cart and filled it with raw meat and beer. Practically wiped the place out. The whole time I'm pushing the cart around, my stomach is going crazy, like it senses what's nearby and it can't handle the wait. It got so strong that I stopped in one of the aisles and, once I was sure nobody was looking, I peeled back the wrapping on a pack of hamburger and tossed a handful into my mouth."

"Gross."

"Everybody has different tastes, bro."

"Uh huh."

"Then I went to check-out and the cashier made some crack, like, 'oooh, looks like someone's having a cookout!' but I just went along with it, too embarrassed to admit it was actually all for me."

"Embarrassed?"

"It was a *lot* of meat." Justin rubbed his stomach and grinned, caught up in the memory. "I ended up eating it all that night, too. We're talking like almost a hundred bucks' worth of meat, dude. Didn't even cook it. Just turned on the TV when I got home and…a few hours later, I was sitting on the floor, stomach feeling like it was about to burst, face covered in specks of hamburger. I know I probably should have felt disgusted with myself, but dude, I'd never felt more satisfied in my life."

"How are you even alive right now?"

He slapped his gut. "Werewolves comes with one hell of a digestive system. You got no idea, man. I ate, like, double my goddamn weight and, somehow, I was still able to get up and take a shower. I mean, yeah, all that meat had tasted great and all, but it also made me realize I hadn't bathed in almost a month."

"Was that unusual for you, though?"

"I don't know, Teddy. Is it unusual for you not to be a total dick?"

"Shelly might say so."

Justin got quiet. The room felt heavier, like a curtain had been thrown over it. He cleared his throat and rubbed his eyes and spat blood out on the floor. Ted continued pretending like he didn't see it. "All right, so I shower and get out, and dude, I don't even know how to begin describing how awesome I felt. That whole month, I'd felt like shit. No energy. Depressed. Fucking exhausted. Then I binge all this meat—"

"—*raw* meat."

"Yeah, all this *raw* meat, and it, like, completely rejuvenated me. I felt like some athlete, which is saying a lot for a guy who's never done a lick of sports in his life, unless you count running from the cops."

"Or dog fighting."

"Fuck you." Justin flashed him the bird then quickly scratched his face, like it was all one natural movement. "But who would have thought, all that time, all I'd needed to feel better was to eat? I didn't know what to do with myself. I was restless. Restless and…well, really horny."

"Uh…" Ted scooted a few inches away.

Justin sighed. "Don't make this weird."

"I…me? You don't want *me* to make this weird?"

"Just listen to my story like a fucking adult, would you?"

"Fine. You're horny. I assume you then jerked off. Really important details you're giving me. I don't know how I could have gone on without knowing these things."

"In retrospect, jerking off would've been the wise move. But no. I wanted something more than just my hand. I hadn't had sex in…well, a long time, okay. And the way I was feeling after my meat buffet, there was no way I could settle for the same shit again. I felt like I could have anything in the world, if I wanted it. So I got a hooker."

"A hooker."

"Yup."

"Jesus Christ." Ted grabbed the top of the deep freezer and pulled himself to his feet, stretching out his spine.

"How? Like, did you just drive around until you found a girl standing on the sidewalk without a lot of clothes on?"

Justin snickered. "You got no inkling how the real world works, do you?"

"Not when it comes to prostitution. I guess not."

"They got apps now, for that kind of stuff."

"Apps?"

Justin nodded.

"What, like Tinder?"

"No, not like Tinder. You don't pay anybody to fuck you on Tinder. There are other apps, specifically to hire escorts."

"How is that legal?" Ted hated himself for being so curious. He wondered what Shelly would think if she could hear him asking these questions. Probably the same things she was already thinking, back at her mother's house.

"It's *not* legal. But since when has that ever stopped anybody?"

"Surely the police are aware of these apps."

"Yeah, of course they are—but, like, the hookers don't come right out and say they'll suck your dick for this amount of money, or whatever. They're sneaky about it. A lot of the apps play up that whole sugar daddy thing."

"Sugar daddy?"

"Uh-huh. Like, they advertise they'll spend time with you if you buy them stuff. No mention of sex at all, but I mean, obviously it's implied."

"So, you used a sugar daddy website."

"I was lonely. Stop laughing, you asshole."

"I'm sorry. It's just that I never in a million years would have imagined you being someone's sugar daddy."

"It's all pretend. It's not like I went out and bought some chick a diamond necklace so she'd blow me on my private yacht. No, how it goes is, first you set up your account and they run a background check before you're even allowed to access any of the features. You know, to make sure you aren't some fuckin' registered sex offender or whatever."

"Seems like a smart idea."

"Oh, most definitely. I'm not complaining at all. Just telling you their process. But yeah, it typically takes a couple days—the background check—but once you're in the clear, the app searches your location and brings up a collection of local girls who are available. You scroll through who's listed and swipe the one you like. So I'm looking through this…expansive library of ladies and—"

"Wait. This is all the same night?"

"What?"

"You're scrolling through the women the same night of the grocery store and the shower?"

"Yeah, it's the same night. So what?"

"I thought you just said it takes a couple days for them to perform a background check."

"Oh. Well, yeah, but I was already a member."

"Jesus. How long have you been hiring prostitutes?"

"I don't see how that's any of your goddamn business, Teddy. There ain't nothing wrong with hookers. They make good fuckin' money, let me tell ya. You don't need to worry about them."

"I'm more worried about you."

"What? Because I fuck hookers? It's twenty-seventeen. Don't be such a goddamn prude."

"I'm not being a prude, it's just that…is that really healthy?"

"Yes, Mom, I use protection."

"No. I mean *mentally*. Don't you want an actual relationship? Someone to come home to at night?"

Justin laughed and snot shot from his nose. He used his bed sheet to wipe it off. "C'mon, Teddy. You honestly think you got room to start giving love advice? Really?"

"What the hell is that supposed to mean?"

Justin raised his brow and stared at him, but didn't respond, just waited for Ted to answer his own question.

"If you think you know something, spit it out."

"I know Shelly left you."

"You don't know shit."

"You've checked your phone every five seconds since you got here, yet you still haven't gotten a single message."

"That doesn't mean anything."

"It means life at home ain't exactly paradise."

Ted resisted the urge to break down and scream a series of obscenities. It was not a new urge. He snapped his fingers. "Just tell me your hooker story and get this crap over with. I'm getting tired."

"You and me both, brother."

TWENTY-THREE

"I WISH I COULD SHOW YOU A PIC OF THIS GIRL, MAN, you got no idea. One look and you'd be coming in your pants."

"Maybe it's a good thing I can't look then."

"Seriously. I'm talking like *Hollywood* sexy. The kinda girl you see in a movie and think, ain't *no way* nobody in real life looks like that. Except she *did* look like that. And then some."

"Wow."

"I'm telling you, Teddy, as soon as I saw her pic on my phone, I immediately forgot about all the crazy shit that'd been happening to me. It was like none of it mattered. I swiped yes and she contacted me like ten minutes later. She wanted to meet up at this motel room off the interstate but I really did not want to leave, so I convinced her to come over here to the house. It felt like ordering takeout, almost."

"That's a really disgusting comparison."

"Because before that, I've been the model for outstanding behavior." He picked his nose and flicked a booger across the room to further prove his point. Ted barely dodged the incoming projectile. "So later that night, she shows up. Of course, she gets lost along the way and has to call for directions, but she eventually finds me. Knocks on the back door and I open it and take one look at her and I'm speechless. I let her inside and she walks upstairs all slowly, letting her ass bounce back and forth in this real tight skirt, knowing full well I'm down on the landing practically hypnotized by the sight of her. But that's what I'm paying for, right? So I follow her up to the kitchen, already sporting the biggest woody you've ever seen, which I'm sure is saying a lot considering who I'm talking to."

"Why are you telling me this?"

Justin caressed his temple with his fist. "Because, asshole, there was a full moon that night. I fucking killed her."

"The prostitute?"

"Yeah."

"How?"

"How the fuck do you think?"

"I…I don't know." But of course he knew.

"We were having a good time. A really good time. One of the best nights of my life. Everything was perfect until it wasn't. I woke up the next day and…and she was dead. But not just dead. It was much more extreme than that. She'd been fuckin' *slaughtered*. Pieces of her were scattered all throughout the guest bedroom upstairs. I swear to god, it was like a *Hellraiser* movie. Only it was all right there in my face. It was real, Teddy. It was so fucking real."

"She was…she was *scattered*?" It was no longer a question of *if* Ted would puke, but *when*.

He nodded, eyes closed. "Teddy. Jesus Christ, man. I don't even know. It was like all my energy and strength had been stored in this balloon, right, and at the sight of her… her *remains*, the balloon popped and my entire will to live deflated. I collapsed to my knees in a puddle of blood that wasn't even wet anymore. It was thick and dry like...hell, I don't know, I guess kind of like oatmeal."

"It was coagulated." Just saying the word made Ted lightheaded.

Justin snapped his fingers and pointed at him. "Yeah! Fuckin' *coagulated*, man. That's exactly right."

"What—what did you do?"

"I'll be honest. Right then, I gave up. I fell face-first into the blood and bits of gore and I bawled like a baby. I was helpless, man. There was nobody I could talk to. All I wanted was to hold my mom's hand and for her to tell me everything was going to be all right. I'd never wanted anything more in my life than that. Jesus fucking Christ. I can't even remember the girl's name. The prostitute. How fucking pathetic is that? Not only did I fuck her, but I also murdered her. I ate her goddamn flesh. And I can't remember her name? Tell me how I deserve to keep living, Teddy. Fucking *tell* me."

"Are you sure you...you ate her?"

"My teeth were stained red."

"Oh."

"I'm a monster. It's okay to say it."

"You're not a monster."

"Then what am I?"

"You're my friend. No matter what you may have done, you're still my friend. And besides, you can't say for sure you know what's happening when you blackout. You can't give up hope like that." Ted didn't believe a word he said, but he felt like it was what Justin needed to hear. If anything Justin had said tonight was the truth, then he probably *was* a monster. Maybe not a werewolf, but a monster nonetheless.

"Come on. It doesn't exactly look promising."

"No." Ted sighed. "It doesn't."

"Give me your word you'll put me down. If I turn. Silver bullet to the heart. Not the head. Not the stomach. Not the dick. Only the heart." He lightly tapped his chest. "Please."

"I can't do that. You know I can't do that." It didn't matter what evil Justin claimed responsibility for: Ted would never actually use the gun. He would continue humoring him for the night, this last night they'd ever spend together, and then he would call the police and tell them everything he knew. Justin needed professional mental help, which Ted could never offer. Not even with a bullet.

"Teddy." Justin slapped himself across the face with an opened palm and grinded his teeth together. "We've been through this. You can't turn me in, otherwise you're gonna have just as much blood on your hands as I do. You don't end the job now, then who knows how many other people I'll kill? No. Not just kill. *Slaughter.*"

"You'll be safe. You won't be able to hurt anybody."

"That's bullshit. I'll only be safe when I'm no longer breathing."

Ted could no longer hold in his breath. "Then why did you even call me?"

He appeared genuinely confused. "What?"

"If you're so determined to die tonight, why bother calling me? Why not just do it yourself? You got hands, don't you? Take the gun, press the barrel against your chest, and pull the trigger. *Bang.* That would have been the end of it. But no. For some reason, you dragged me into your fucking mess, and I don't understand why."

"Teddy, I—"

"Did you honestly think, for a single second, that I would ever seriously agree to shoot you?"

"Well, yeah."

"Flip the situation around. Would you shoot *me* if I thought I was some...some fucking *wolfman*?"

"I'd like to think so, yeah." He nodded.

"Sure. You would *like* to think so, but I know damn well you wouldn't. Because you're a good person. You're a good friend. You would listen to my insane ramblings, you would give me the space I needed to vent, but then you would make a call and get me the real help I needed. Just like I'm gonna do for you. And you may not like it. No. Let's be honest. You'll probably hate me for it. But this is what needs to be done. So go ahead and hate me, but think about why you're hating me. Because I won't *shoot* you. Because I'm trying to fucking *help* you get better."

Justin lowered his head and didn't respond. They sat in the basement, silent save for the sounds of their heavy breathing and the constant hum of the deep freezer. Ted gave some thought to putting an end to this charade now and calling the police, but it was close enough to midnight at this point that he might as well let Justin have this one thing. Give him until midnight, just to prove that he wasn't going to transform into some ridiculous creature, then tell him a deal was a deal and get the rest over with. It would be rough, watching him carted off to some padded room, but it wasn't like Ted was left with much choice. It was either that or actually shoot him, which obviously wasn't about to happen.

He wished like hell he could talk to Shelly about what was going on. She'd know what to do. She always had the perfect solution to every problem. Which, unfortunately, explained why she refused to answer his calls or respond to his texts. Fuck. He should've just knocked on her mother's door. What was the worst that would have happen? Instead, he was stuck in a basement listening to his childhood best friend talk about werewolves. This was not how Ted had intended the day to end. Sitting in front of his mother-in-law's house, he'd gone through the various apologies he could offer to convince Shelly to forgive him and come back home. In retrospect, he doubted any of them would have come close to working. If anything, he would have only ended up pissing her off even further. It was best to keep his distance, at least until she decided to reach out to him. But it was hard. It was so goddamn hard. All he knew in life was Shelly, and now she was gone. Temporarily or permanently, he didn't know which. Jesus Christ, please let it only be temporary. He would lose his mind if she left him for good this time. He'd end up like Justin, chained to a stolen ship anchor with a bull's-eye painted on his chest.

Ted tried to resist glancing at the revolver on the floor and failed. Two bullets, not one. It was difficult not to obsess about the number. One for each of them. An intentional decision? Ted had his suspicions, but he feared voicing them would only result with him sounding just as crazy as Justin. Ted didn't want to shoot *anybody*, but the more he thought about Shelly, the less irrational the idea sounded.

Justin's head was still tilted down as he sat against the anchor. Maybe he'd fallen asleep. Maybe he was about to transform into a wolf.

Ted pointed at him. "Those chains starting to hurt yet?"

Justin shrugged and raised his head, yawning. "They're digging into my skin a little bit."

"Want me to unlock you so we can loosen them?"

"No." He grabbed one of the chains and pulled it tighter against his stomach. "If anything, I deserve much worse."

"Tell me something."

"I'll try."

"Why the heart?"

"What?"

"Why do you have to be shot in the heart? Why can't it be anywhere? I don't remember anything about it being the heart in movies."

"Oh. Well, I posted a question on Yahoo! Answers—you know, about the best way to put down a werewolf?—and the general consensus seemed to agree that the heart was the way to go. The silver's supposed to prevent…uh, what is it? *Regeneration*. So, like, if you get shot in the head, it ain't guaranteed you'll die, right? People survive head-shots all the time. But a shot to the heart? Oh, baby. You're fuckin' *gone*. Although, to be fair, the heart thing wasn't the most *upvoted* answer, but it *was* the most frequently commented. The most upvoted answer, on the other hand, involved fucking my mother with a silver crucifix, which didn't really seem like it'd be very effective, given how she's dead and all."

"Jesus fucking Christ."

"What?"

Ted burst out laughing. There was no stopping it. Justin stared at him in confusion. Ted's laughter quickly spiraled into silent sobs. He wiped his eyes and sat in silence for a while, then cleared his throat. "I cheated on Shelly."

Justin dropped the chain he'd been pulling. "What?"

"You were right. Shelly did leave me. I haven't heard from her in almost two days and I'm terrified I'm never going to again."

"Oh."

"I started seeing this girl at work. We'd been friends for a while. Usually had the same lunch schedule, so we'd eat together. I don't know how it happened. I'm so fucking stupid."

"How did Shelly find out?"

"We got caught. At…work. We were messing around in a closet and a supervisor walked in on us. Fired us both on the spot. Word spread and it didn't take long to reach Shelly." Ted paused, studying the way his fingers were shaking. "To be honest, I think she suspected I was cheating on her for a while. She just didn't want to come out and say anything."

"Why do you say that?"

"Just, you know, the way she'd act around me. The last couple months, it's felt like we were roommates instead of husband and wife. It was weird. I don't know. Maybe she hadn't suspected anything. But she's smart, and I'm not. She can pick up on things."

"So she found out and then, what, told you the marriage was over and left?"

"She said she needed some time to think, and to leave her alone until she was ready to contact me."

"And have you?"

Ted emitted a nervous laugh and held up his phone. "I've been calling and texting nonstop. I can't stop myself. I…I think I'm losing my mind."

"I guess that makes two of us, then."

"I don't know what I'm going to do if she divorces me. I just don't know."

"You remember that night, back when we were just kids? The night Shelly and Jessica slept over and we watched *An American Werewolf in London* and debuted our jizz."

Ted grimaced, but reluctantly nodded. "Of course I remember it."

"I think, maybe, that might have been the best night of my life. What about you?"

"Yeah. I think I'd agree."

"What if everybody only gets one real, *best* night, and that night was ours? Would that mean everything afterward was just extra? Like a scene after the credits. Sometimes it's good and sometimes it's bad, but in the grand scheme of things, it doesn't truly matter all that much."

"What are you talking about?"

"Maybe our lives peaked that night we watched *American Werewolf*, and we should just be grateful for all the time we've been allowed to have since. If Shelly left you, maybe that's okay."

"What?"

"You two have been together for a long-ass time. Not everything lasts forever, right? Sometimes things need to drift apart. People split. It's the natural flow of humanity."

"Fuck you, man. I don't even know what you're saying but fuck you, anyway."

"What I'm saying is, maybe we weren't meant to live past fourteen. Maybe we expired the night we became men, but nobody noticed and we kept on living, slowly rotting like fruit forgotten in the fridge. And now there's a new motherfucker in charge of this shit, and he discovered this...this *discrepancy* that is our lives, and he's come to collect what's owed."

"Jesus fucking Christ." Ted stood and wiped drool from his lips. He gave Justin one last glance before pulling out his cell phone. "You really are nuts, you know that?"

"What are you doing?"

"What I should've done hours ago."

"Teddy. Come on, brother. Don't do this."

"It's already done."

Ted dialed 9-1-1 and pressed the phone against his ear.

TWENTY-FOUR

"Goddammit." Ted hung up and squeezed the phone with his fist.

Justin paused his temper tantrum. "What? What's wrong?"

"The service in this basement is bullshit."

"Give me until midnight, Teddy. Please." He reached out and grasped at open air.

It was possible the lack of service had been some kind of sign indicating he should wait to call. But nobody had ever had much service down here, and in Ted's panic, he'd forgotten this fact. It didn't mean that he wasn't supposed to call the police. It just meant that he'd have to leave the basement first.

Or he could sit back down on the ground and wait out the rest of the clock. Except he didn't think he could. Not anymore. If he had to listen to Justin say one more crazy-ass thing, he'd use up both of the silver bullets on himself and leave Justin chained there until starvation ate him from the inside out.

Ted tried to apologize again, but found he lacked the ability to even meet Justin in the eyes anymore. He turned around and walked out of the basement, phone raised, waiting for the signal bar to reappear. Justin screamed his name and begged him to come back. Screamed so loud Ted couldn't hear himself think. He stood on the landing between the basement and the stairs and hovered his thumb above the 9 on his touchscreen. It would only take four taps to put an end to all of this. One to the 9, two to the 1, then one final blow to the green CALL button.

Footsteps creaked from outside somewhere on the back porch. He returned the cell to his pocket and peeked out through the curtain. A shadow moved quickly through the darkness, approaching the back door. Ted released the curtain and stepped away just as the door shot open. The frame smashed into his shoulder and knocked him down the couple steps leading from the landing to the basement. He tumbled to the floor and banged his hand against the wall. He looked up and saw a large muscular man in dirty overalls standing above him, murder in his eyes.

"You Justin?"

"Wh-what do you want?"

The man kicked Ted in the ribs. Ted groaned and curled into the fetal position, spit and vomit spraying out of his mouth. Embarrassment hit him before the pain. The man grimaced and backed away.

"For the love of God, get up and fight like a man."

"Why...do you want to fight me?" It sounded more like a whine than he would have preferred, but it was an honest question. He'd never seen this guy in his life.

Justin continued his screaming from the bedroom. "Teddy! What the fuck is going on!"

The man ignored Ted and followed the sound of the voice, slowly edging toward the bedroom and stopping outside the doorway, pressing his back against the wall.

"Who's there? Get out here right now."

Justin paused for a moment and Ted feared he'd never respond. "Who the fuck is that?"

"I'm the motherfucker who's gonna kick your ass, if you're who I think you are, bitch."

"Where's Teddy?"

The man stopped and glanced back at Ted, then smirked. "Teddy's busy."

"What the fuck did you do to him? What do you want?"

"Come out here and we'll talk about what I want."

"Well, that ain't fuckin' happening." Justin fell into a coughing fit that lasted long enough for both Ted and the strange man to show concern. He recovered half a minute later and spit something disgusting against cement. "So, you police or what?"

"Nah, man. I ain't the fuckin' cops."

"Then what the hell?" Justin paused, thinking. "Oh, wait. Are you looking for Donny?"

"Man, I don't know no fuckin' Donny. Get the fuck out here before you make me drag you out."

"Go fuck yourself, asshole." Justin cleared his throat. "Teddy! What the hell's going on? Are you okay?"

When Ted spoke, a hot pain shot through his stomach. "He just busted in through the back door. I don't know who he is."

The man turned around and stomped toward Ted. "No one asked you to speak."

Ted held out his hands and mouthed the word "no" over and over but the man didn't seem to hear him. He kicked Ted again, this time in the head. Something wet blurred his vision and his nose no longer felt like it was completely connected to his face. He rolled over on his stomach and held his face as blood streamed between his fingers. He wondered where his phone had gone. He'd thrown it somewhere while tumbling down the steps. It might as well had landed in fucking Africa.

He lifted his face from his hands and saw the man walking back to the bedroom, again stopping at the doorway. "Let me guess. You got a piece in there and you're just waiting for me to walk through so you can plug me. That true? You fuckin' strapped?"

"Uh. Nothing within reach." Justin giggled, then coughed again.

"Because I came with just my fists. You prepared to do the same?"

"Dude. Why are you so mad at me?"

The man leaned against the wall and inhaled a deep, contemplative breath. "Let me tell you a story."

Justin laughed and groaned all in one gargled mess of a sound. "Dude, all we've been fuckin' doing tonight is telling stories. Give us a break."

"No. I think you'll wanna hear this one. Trust me."

Justin didn't respond, but when it became clear the man wasn't going to continue until he did, he sighed. "Well, shit. Go on, then. No one's fuckin' stopping you, are they?"

"I work down at the mill. All day, I'm busting my ass, sweating through my uniform, getting bits of metal and shit stuck in my skin. And why do I do it? To support my family. My woman. My boy. They're everything to me. Do you understand that? They're everything. When I get home at night, all I want to do is spend time with my family. Just like any man worth a damn."

"Dude, what in all of the motherfucks does this have to do with me?"

Ted started to slowly crawl toward the bedroom, careful not to draw attention of the man standing at the doorway. Whatever was about to happen wouldn't be good, and considering Justin was chained to a goddamn anchor, it would unfortunately be up to Ted to do something about it, whatever the hell that meant.

The man slapped the wall. "Tonight I get home, and I find my boy out in the back yard, snot and tears all over his face. Kid's been crying for hours."

"Sounds like your wife should probably look after him better."

He paused, grinding his teeth together. "So I find him like this in the back yard, minutes after I get home, and I kneel down and I ask him, 'Dylan, buddy, what's wrong? What's the trouble?' And he says he's not allowed to tell me, because the man down the street said he'd get in trouble if anybody found out."

"Oh, shit."

"Now, you can imagine my fuckin' surprise. You can guess what I'm thinking. But I question him some more, and I find out it's not even that—trust me, bitch, if it had been, you'd already be dead, there wouldn't be no fuckin' story time. My son, he tells me the man down the street has been paying him money to kill animals and bring him the corpses. But today, he refused to pay. He told him to go away. My boy, oh my God, you should have seen how sad he was. He thought the man down the street was mad at him, thought that he was doing a bad job, that he's no good at anything. And I ask my boy, 'Dylan, what the hell is this man doing with these animals?' But even he don't know that. And you know what? I don't really fucking care. Maybe you're screwing them. Whatever. You wanna be a sick fuck, you can be a sick fuck. That's your right. But you messed up by dragging my boy into all this shit. So, you understand, I gotta kick your ass now. I won't kill ya. He promised me you never touched him, and I believe that. But I still gotta make you bleed. I still gotta teach you a lesson. Now you either come out here with your hands up so I know you ain't packin', or I'm gonna come in there, but if I gotta do that, I'm gonna make sure you spend the rest of your life with a limp."

Justin was silent for a moment. "Some people are sexually turned on by limps, you know."

The man shook his head, taking quick breaths, pumping himself up, then entered the bedroom. He stopped just inside the room and stared at Justin chained to the ship anchor, hysterical.

"What the fuck?"

Ted didn't give him a chance to react. It was better to get him now, while he was confused and vulnerable. He rushed from behind and tackled the man with every ounce of strength he could gather. Together they fell to the floor and bounced off the cement. Ted kept his grip around him the whole way down, but the man easily broke loose once inertia finished its work.

He scrambled away. "Get the fuck off of me."

Ted lunged at him again, not sure what he was even doing. Justin cheered his name. "Kick his ass, Teddy!" Weirdly enough, his encouragement seemed to spike his adrenaline. Ted hadn't been in a fight since high school. This was crazy. If Shelly saw him right now, she would take him back just so she could leave him all over again. But then again, if Shelly *was* here right now, he probably wouldn't be fighting some stranger. She would know how to solve the issue without resorting to violence. Or maybe it would turn her on. He didn't know.

But she wasn't here, so what did it matter?

The man clocked Ted good in the jaw and knocked him flat on his back. All at once, his short-lived confidence drained away. He lay motionless on the floor and waited for the man to flee the basement, most likely in search of a phone to call the police and tell them all about the weird set-up happening in Justin's basement. Imagining the phone call made Ted laugh despite the pain consuming the entirety of his body with the tenacity of a python savoring a fresh kill. What would he report first: his son getting paid to kill stray animals, the naked man chained to a ship anchor, or the other man who tackled him to prevent his escape? Any one of them would surely do the trick.

But the man chose not to flee and instead leaped onto Ted, crushing his stomach and making him momentarily forget how to breathe. Ted raised his hands to protect his face, but they did no good against the man's fists raining upon him. Each blow flicked the lights off and on in Ted's head. He wondered if he was about to die, if this stranger was going to kill him right here in Justin's disgusting basement. And for what? He wasn't even sure, truth be told. None of this shit had anything to do with him.

Somewhere, a million miles away, Justin screamed Ted's name.

Ted gave up trying to block his face and dropped both arms to the floor. He saw brief flashes of the man on top of him. The look in his eyes didn't seem human. The man had snapped. He wasn't going to stop hitting Ted until someone pulled him off, and the only other person in the house wasn't exactly about to help out anytime soon.

Ted's hand touched something cold. Something made of steel.

The conscious decision to lift the revolver never arrived. First he touched the gun, then time skipped a beat and the gun was somehow in his hand and his finger was curling around the trigger and the universe exploded with a deafening boom.

Everything went dark for a moment, and when Ted managed to open his eyes again, the man was sitting across the room next to the doorway, one hand holding his stomach as it gushed a steady flow of blood.

"You shot me. Mother...fucker. *You fucking shot*—"

Then he stopped talking, and a few seconds later he stopped breathing, too.

TWENTY-FIVE

TED DROPPED THE REVOLVER. IF IT MADE A SOUND when it bounced against the floor, he didn't hear it. A sharp ringing flooded his eardrums and threatened to split his skull in half. The gunshot lingered, its aftermath eternal. He wanted to look at Justin and beg him to tell him this wasn't really happening, but he couldn't take his eyes off the man he'd just shot. The man who now sat across from him, motionless.

Dead.

No. He didn't even know this guy. Ten minutes ago he didn't exist. Now here he was. Dead. Dead because of Ted, whether he wanted to admit it or not. He'd pulled the trigger. Yes, he hadn't had much choice, but that didn't make him any less guilty of ending the man's life. Ted never had to tackle him. He could have just slipped out the back door and let him and Justin settle their argument alone.

But that's not what happened. He had tried to help. For once in his life, he actually threw himself into danger to help a friend. And it ended with him murdering a stranger.

"Jesus fucking Christ." Saying something aloud broke the spell and Ted managed to briefly look elsewhere. Justin sat on the mattress, still hypnotized by their new guest.

Except it was different somehow. Justin didn't seem to be looking at the corpse with horror or disgust or anything like that. Justin's eyes were focused, determined. He stared at the man with desire.

He licked his lips.

Ted gagged and shook his head. "What the fuck? What the fuck? I can't do this. I can't fucking do this."

Justin looked up at him with genuine confusion. "Huh? You can't do what?"

"I just fucking killed somebody. I just...I just..."

Justin shrugged. "It was self-defense. Relax. He hit you first."

"No, no, no." Ted paced the room, careful to steer clear of the body against the wall. "That still doesn't give me the right to...to fucking *shoot* somebody. Oh my god. Oh my fucking—I...I fucking killed him, didn't I? I killed him. Who the fuck—who the fuck even is he? Oh my god. Holy shit."

"Honestly, dude. If you haven't done what you did, who knows what he was capable of. That guy came here to fuck us up. Hell, look at your face. He already fucked you up, and it didn't seem like he was planning on stopping any time soon."

"I killed him."

"Sometimes people die. It's okay. It happens to everybody, eventually."

"Justin. I fucking killed him."

"You're gonna be fine."

Ted stopped pacing, both hands in the midst of yanking hair from skull. "What are you even talking about? You're crazy. You think you're a fucking werewolf! What do you know? Nothing is going to be fine. I just fucking killed a man and I don't even know his name and you're telling me it's going to be fine? Fuck you. Nothing is ever going to be fine again."

"Look. Nobody knows you're here, right?"

Ted thought about lying, but what would be the point? "No one knows."

"Well, do you think I'm gonna snitch? As far as anybody knows, we haven't talked in years."

"But you called me. The cell phone records will show that."

"So what? They won't know what we talked about. They won't know you came over. Let's just keep sticking with our plan, okay? Just when you dispose of my body, throw this asshole in with me. Nobody will know. Sure, that fuckin' snitch Dylan might tell the police about me. But guess what? I'll be gone, too. Plus, he's like ten. Ten-year-olds don't know shit about shit. Cops won't have nothing to interrogate but their own itty bitty dicks."

Ted could barely comprehend what he was hearing. "What...what are you talking about? I'm not *disposing* of your goddamn body because I'm not fucking killing you. Why can't you get that through your thick skull?" He turned and accidentally saw the man against the wall again. His lap was drenched in blood and his jaw hung open in a silent, frozen scream. "Goddammit, goddammit, *goddammit.*"

"What time is it?"

"Oh, who fucking cares?"

"Teddy. Come on. What time is it?"

Ted sighed and reached into his pocket for his cell phone but came up empty. Recollection hit him. He'd dropped it while falling down the stairs. Fear seized him as paranoia tried its best to convince him Shelly had tried calling while he was busy murdering somebody. He walked out of the room, holding his breath as he passed the dead man. It couldn't have gone far.

"Teddy! Teddy, come back. Please don't leave. Teddy!"

"Shut up. I'm looking for my phone."

"Oh."

It had slid into the bathroom. He found it next to the shower, upside down. Flipping it over revealed a cracked but still functioning screen. The time read 11:32. No missed calls. No unread messages. Nobody had tried contacting him. Nobody gave a shit.

Justin shouted his name from the bedroom, but Ted remained quiet, staring at the cracked screen and its lack of notifications. Even his email was empty. Usually he couldn't go more than an hour without receiving some kind of penis-enlargement advertisement. Maybe the low signal simply hadn't allowed his service to refresh. Shelly could have been calling him all night and he wouldn't have known. Panic pushed him out of the bathroom and dragged him upstairs. He stomped loud and fast, inspiring another round of screaming from Justin, worried about getting abandoned down in the basement. Ted offered no words of reassurance. He couldn't promise he wasn't about to abandon him. He couldn't promise anything right now. He'd just taken the life of another man. Anything was fucking possible.

He lifted his cell phone high above his head as he wandered around the house, waiting for more signal bars to generate. They blinked in and out of existence. They did not want to be here in this house of death and Ted didn't blame them.

Justin's screams were muffled by the floorboards. It

sounded almost tolerable, compared to what was actually waiting down there for him. He yearned for another beer, but the fridge had long been empty. He briefly entertained the idea of going out and picking up a six-pack. Would he return? Doubtful. Once Ted left this house there was no goddamn way he was ever coming back. He was done.

A door in the dining area caught his eye and he lowered the cell phone. The guest bedroom. He hadn't seen it in years. Even when they were kids, Ted hardly spent time upstairs. Why bother when everything they could ever need could be found in the basement? Life had been good down there once. It'd served as a catacomb of good memories. After tonight, all those memories were ruined. Destroyed. A perfect crop flung into the sky by a passing tornado. There was no longer anything worth salvaging.

Ted reached out for the guest room door handle and paused, replaying Justin's words about the woman he'd supposedly killed.

("Pieces of her were scattered all throughout the guest bedroom upstairs.")

He turned the knob and opened the door and held his breath, expecting to walk in on a crime scene straight from a horror movie despite all logic trying desperately to convince him this was all bullshit.

The room seemed fine. Not spotless, but also not spattered with the gore of a slaughtered woman. Ted sat at the edge of the bed and closed his eyes. He thought about laying back and taking a nap. Would the situation have improved by the time he awoke? Probably not, but good ideas were limited tonight. Anything and nothing seemed worth trying at this point.

He glanced down at his phone and still no new notifications had updated. Fuck it. Fuck everything. He turned and went to rest his phone on the nightstand but stopped when he discovered another phone already there, connected to a white cord plugged into the wall outlet.

The phone was protected in a red case decorated with glitter and ladybugs.

Ted recognized the case. Of course he did.

He'd bought it for Shelly two years ago.

It wasn't real. It couldn't be. The phone was simply a mirage. Like how people lost in the desert hallucinate water. Dehydrated and disoriented. Ted's sanity cracked. It made sense that he'd start seeing shit that wasn't really there. He set his own phone on the bed and reached his free hand to the nightstand, hoping it'd wave through the other phone like it was a hologram.

The phone was real.

He unplugged it and powered it on. Ten seconds passed as he waited for it to spring to life. Ten seconds that felt like ten years. His heart skipped at the number of unread text messages blinking at the bottom of the screen. He couldn't bring himself to look at them, to read the pathetic things he'd texted her since she left.

Since she left.

Ted's phone dinged and it startled him enough to drop Shelly's. Hesitant, he peeked across the bed. Two notifications had updated on his phone. One missed call. One unheard voicemail message.

Not from Shelly, but her mother.

His arm was shaking as he pressed PLAY and raised it to his ear.

"Is she with you? Please. I just need to know that she's safe. She went out last night and never came back. She didn't call or

text to let me know what was going on. I'm just worried, is all. I know you two have been having trouble, so hopefully you've made up and everything is fine now. Please call me as soon as you can. Thank you."

Ted fell off the bed and landed on his knees. Vomit worked its way up his throat. He opened his mouth and a thick stream of beer and cheeseburgers sprayed across the carpet.

Afterward, he collapsed next to the puddle and struggled to control his breathing. If his heart continued beating at this pace it would burst through his chest. The smell of his vomit influenced another spell of sickness. He wiped his mouth and sat up and stared at the puddle, grimacing. Without standing, he pulled down the bed sheet from the mattress above him and threw it over the vomit. He covered it less for Justin's benefit and more for himself. Nobody wanted to look at vomit—*anybody's* vomit.

He leaned his head back against the wall and sighed. Exhausted. Drained yet full of questions. Questions he probably already knew the answers to but refused to admit.

It took him a minute to notice the mattress, now bare of a sheet.

It was stained red.

Somebody had bled on this mattress.

Somebody had bled a lot.

Fuck.

Fuck fuck fuck.

Ted collected the two phones and stormed through the house and down the stairs, fueled by rage. Justin hadn't moved from the mattress, although it looked like he'd certainly tried. He lay across it, drenched in sweat, gasping for breath. He barely possessed enough energy to lift his head upon Ted's arrival.

"Teddy…you came back. I thought you'd left me."

Instead of saying anything, Ted just raised Shelly's cell phone and waited. Electricity flowed through his body. He was going to explode.

The relief vanished from Justin's face as he shot up. "Teddy, now Teddy…" He stood and tried walking forward but the chain pulled him back. "Goddammit, Teddy, you gotta listen to me, okay, man? You gotta—"

Ted tried to talk with authority but his voice came out weak and frightened. "Why…why do you have Shelly's phone?" Tears streamed down his eyes as his vocals squeaked. "Oh, goddammit, *why* do you have her *phone? Why do you have her phone? Why?*"

"I was going to tell you, I swear to fucking god, okay? I was building up to it. I fucking promise I was going to tell you. I was waiting until midnight, in case you still had doubts…"

"*Why do you have my wife's phone?*"

"Teddy, please, let me—"

All concern for the dead guy in the basement vanished. Ted dropped the phone and tackled Justin against the wall. Ted's forehead smashed against the ship anchor and knocked him back, but he kept his arms wrapped around Justin's torso and brought him down with him. Justin didn't attempt to defend himself as Ted sat on top of his stomach and wrapped his hands around his throat and squeezed.

"*Where is my wife? Where is my fucking wife? What did you do with Shelly? What the fuck did you do with Shelly?*"

Justin's eyes widened and his cheeks paled and his neck grew hot and Ted squeezed tighter and screamed louder and saw black dots floating in his vision. He demanded answers Justin couldn't give while being strangled, but he didn't care. Ted no longer possessed control of his body. If his hands wanted to strangle Justin, then that's exactly what they were going to do.

Justin scratched at Ted's arms but there was hardly any fight in him. He was letting this happen. This was what Justin wanted. For Ted to kill him. Not because he was a werewolf. No, that was fucking stupid. But for another reason, yes. A far more sinister one.

Tears spilled down Justin's cheek as his face bloated and still he did not resist. He was really gonna let this happen. Fuck.

Ted released his grip and sat back against the wall, next to him on the dirty mattress. Justin rolled over and fell into an intense coughing fit, wheezing and rasping as he frantically hunted for oxygen. Ted waited for him to recover, plotting his next action. All he could think about was grabbing his throat again. This time maybe he'd just rip his head clean off. Ted wasn't a strong man by nature, but right now he felt like he could shatter the planet with one punch.

Justin stopped coughing eventually and sat next to Ted. "Okay. I deserved that."

"Just…just tell me what happened. Please." He wanted to add an *is she okay?* but feared his reaction to the question more than his actual answer.

"Teddy…" He cleared his throat and wiped his eyes. "Teddy, man. I just want you to know how fucking sorry I am."

Ted refused to meet his eyes. "I'm listening."

TWENTY-SIX

"FOR THE LAST MONTH, THE HUNGER HAS BEEN stronger than it ever has been. It's like, the more time passes, the worse the cravings become. One night I was out walking to Walmart, intending to stock up on raw meat. I didn't want to drive. I don't know. At that point I was so goddamn fidgety, being behind the wheel seemed like torture, you know? No way I could sit still that long. So I was walking, and I stumbled across this kid in the road, hunched over a dead possum. You've already met the kid. And, uh, his father, I guess. I asked him what he thought about that there roadkill and he gave me the typical 'oh my god, it's so cool'. One thing led to another and we struck up a deal. Any time he finds something dead on the side of the road—or anywhere, really, what the fuck do I care where he gets it from, right?—he'd bring it to me and I'd give him a little bit of cash.

"I guess I figured eating dead animals would be better than what I...what I really wanted to do. What I woke up in the middle of the night drooling about. I thought maybe if I kept forcing this shit down my throat, it'd satisfy the cravings. Don't think I enjoyed any of it because I didn't. The shit was gross. But I still stuck with it for about a month, and it did nothing to help my problem. It did nothing to…to *sate* my appetite. Like eating celery or some bullshit.

"Then, come yesterday morning, I woke up with such an intense pain in my gut, I doubled over the toilet and started vomiting blood. My whole goddamn body felt like it was on fire. A few years back I had this gas station burrito while driving to Ohio for some show, and the food poisoning I experienced that night was Heaven compared to yesterday. There was only one way to fix this, and I was no longer strong enough to resist. So I…I opened up the app. The escort app. And I started scrolling through the faces, trying to figure out which one would be missed the least, like you could tell such a thing just from their mugshot, right? Ugh. So fucking stupid, I know.

"Anyway. I'm scrolling through the faces, trying to decide who I'm gonna kill—who I'm gonna *eat*—but at the same time praying for some kind of…I don't know, I guess divine intervention. *Anything* to stop me from doing what I'm about to do. Because I don't want to fucking do it, you know? But…the hunger. Teddy. Oh my god. The fucking hunger. It was like that astral projection shit you were talking about. I had no control, man. Just watching from the sidelines. But then something happened. I get a notification—a Facebook message pops up and blocks out the hooker app on my phone. The message, it's from Shelly."

"Why would she message you?"

"I guess she was up late and needing somebody to talk to and she saw I was also online so she just reached out. Asked me if I wanted to get together and catch up. Said she was going through some rough shit with you and her mom was driving her crazy. Said she didn't know what else to do."

"Shut up. Stop."

"So, yeah. I mean, we used to be real close, back in the day and all. She came over pretty much immediately. And weirdly enough, my hunger had kinda numbed for the time being. Like all this time, what I'd needed was a distraction. To be involved in something other than my own stupid bullshit. We sat down at the kitchen table and we cracked open some beers and we talked most of the evening. We caught up on things we'd missed. It was pretty obvious something crazy had been going on with me. Shit, you've seen how I look. Imagine what *she* thought. This was only yesterday for Christ's sake. But I didn't feel it was polite to burden her with my problems. She obviously was troubled enough without hearing about me being some goddamn werewolf. I kept asking her what was wrong and she eventually broke down and started bawling and apologizing. Said you'd lost you job, said you'd lost it because you was fucking around with some other girl at work."

"I…I didn't…it was…"

"She loved you, man. And you broke her heart."

"Stop. Please stop."

"We didn't…we didn't do anything, if that's what you're thinking. She told me she'd left you the day before, that it was all over Facebook and shit, all the drama about you and the girl you was fucking behind her back…it was all too much. She needed to get away. And her mom was driving her nuts. She, uh…she asked if she could stay the night."

"What the fuck did you do?"

"Well, I told her to make herself at home, and I'd go pick up some food since there wasn't shit to eat. This time I took my car. I ordered a pizza, but didn't go there immediately. Instead I just kind of drove around for a while, looking…"

"Looking for what?"

"Looking for my own dinner."

"Oh."

"I found this little dog circling a tree. No tags. He walked right up to me, friendly. I—"

"I don't want to hear this."

"Okay. Well, I'm sure you can imagine what happened. Afterward, I went and picked up the pizza, then got back to the house, and…I found Shelly in the basement. In the same room we're in right now."

"Was the anchor here?"

"Yeah. I've been chaining myself to it every night for a few weeks now. Just in case. But that isn't what she was looking at."

"What was…?"

Justin pointed a trembling finger at the deep freezer in front of them. "The hooker. The one I told you about. The one I…well, you know. The parts I didn't eat while in wolf form, they had to go somewhere."

"It wasn't locked?"

"I wasn't used to having company."

"What…what happened?"

"She freaked out. There was no way I could explain myself. She tried to run away. I…I chased her."

"Stop."

"She would have gone straight to the police. And they sure as fuck wouldn't have listened to anything I had to say. I caught her in the back yard. I dragged her inside the house. Then I…I…"

Ted stood and stared at the deep freezer. "Open it."

"Teddy…"

"Open it."

"You have the key."

"What?"

"The key for my chains works in that lock, too."

Ted found the key in his pocket and tried to insert it into the padlock but his hand was shaking so much he couldn't get it to fit. He paused and breathed in, breathed out, his face hot as lava, his heart a ticking time bomb, and tried again. This time it slid in. Justin tried protesting but he blocked out his voice. His focus narrowed on the lock and trying to take it off, but his hands refused to obey his commands.

It fell to the floor. All he had to do was lift the lid and he'd see what was inside.

He couldn't do it.

Justin was crazy. Delusional. None of this was real.

If that was true, then why couldn't he look inside and prove it?

Fuck.

Ted lifted the lid and immediately closed it. Then he opened it again and stared down inside.

Staring into Shelly's eyes.

Searching for some sign of life beyond her frosted lashes.

Wondering what happened to the rest of her body.

Wishing he didn't already know the answer.

"Teddy? Teddy? Man. Please. I'm so fucking sorry. Teddy, man, please, believe me…I didn't…I didn't mean to… Teddy, fuck, man, I'm sorry, okay? Talk to me, Teddy. Please talk to me."

Ted closed the deep freezer and retrieved the revolver from the floor and took two steps toward the mattress and pressed the barrel against Justin's forehead and pulled the trigger.

TWENTY-SEVEN

TED CALLED 9-1-1 AND TOLD THEM HE'D JUST killed his best friend and sat out on the back porch and waited for them to arrive. He left the revolver in the basement. It was empty, anyway. He made sure of that by turning it upon his own skull and repeatedly triggering empty clicks. If there were more bullets somewhere else, silver or otherwise, Justin had kept them well-hidden.

Ted remained on the porch, listening to distant sirens grow nearer, on their way to accept his invitation. He didn't know what he was going to tell them. The truth seemed impossible but any other explanations were just as unlikely. Justin had developed a mental illness or a brain parasite and, as a result, murdered multiple people, including Ted's wife. In a blind fit of rage, Ted got his revenge. These were the facts. The cops could do with them whatever they pleased. Ted wasn't sure he gave a shit. It was enough of a relief just to be out of the basement.

He thought about calling his mother-in-law and letting her know he'd found her daughter. The idea lasted all of five seconds before he tossed it aside. Let her find out from someone else. Surely she would blame him for this, anyway, and maybe she wouldn't be entirely wrong. Maybe she'd be one hundred percent correct.

This was Ted's fault.

Either directly or indirectly, it would always lead back to him.

So fuck it.

He waited. If he'd been trying to escape before the police arrived, he would have had time to take a shower, eat a meal, and get dressed before fleeing. The response time was pathetic, but it gave him time to think, which perhaps was the worst kind of hell of them all.

They eventually came. Two squad cars pulled up at the same time from either end of the alley. Guns drawn. Leery footsteps crunching through gravel. Ted already had both arms raised, although maybe it would have been better to still have the revolver with him. Point it forward and get rewarded with a burst of lead. Cop suicide. They wouldn't even hesitate.

But he didn't have the revolver anymore so he stayed where he was, arms up, as they approached and handcuffed him. Ted explained the situation, told them where they'd be able to find the bodies.

One of the cops raised his brow. "Bodies? Plural?"

Ted nodded. "Bodies."

"Ah, fuck. Okay, then." He told his partner to stay with Ted and entered the house. A minute later he came back out and vomited in the back yard. The two cops sat with Ted and waited for backup to arrive.

One of the cops lit a cigarette and blew smoke into the night. His wristwatch beeped and he sighed. "Goddamn. Can't believe it's only now twelve. This shift's gonna last forever."

The other cop shrugged and bummed a smoke. "Maybe Jed will let us leave early. Because of trauma and shit."

"Good point. And if we have to fake it a little…"

"I don't think we're gonna have to fake it."

Smoke drifted into Ted's face and he coughed. "Wait. Did…did you say it was midnight?"

One of the cops shoved him and he rolled off the back deck. "Who the fuck told you to speak?"

Ted landed on his back, his handcuffed hands digging into his spine. The cops laughed and threatened more violence if he tried to get up.

He stared up into the sky, at the moon hanging overhead. So bright and full of life. He'd never seen anything so beautiful in his life.

A thought occurred to him then. It was a silly thought, truth be told, but it sent chills through his body all the same. He thought about the target Justin had drawn on his chest, over where his heart ought to be located. Thought about how sometimes people survive headshots. Thought about how they don't always die.

Back inside the house, something howled.

PART 2

ANTE MERIDIEM

TWENTY-EIGHT

"WHAT THE FUCK WAS THAT?"

The cop who hadn't yet gone inside the house withdrew his pistol and pointed it at the back door. "Marv? Did you see a dog in there or some shit?"

The other cop—Marv—shook his head. "Nah, man. I didn't see no fuckin' dogs." He stepped off the deck and kicked Ted in the ribs. "Hey, asshole, you got a dog in there?"

Ted tried to talk but couldn't find the words. No language in this universe could accurately warn them of what awaited inside the house. Hell, *he* didn't even know. Not really. But he could imagine, and what his imagination conjured frightened him stupid.

The howl again, this time longer, more crazed.

"Fuck." The spooked cop shuffled his feet, attention bouncing from Ted to the back door. "That sounds huge."

Marv nodded to the house. "We gotta go in there, don't we?"

"The fuck we do."

"If it's a dog, it might be eating evidence."

The other cop's face paled. "What do you mean *if* it's a dog?"

"You know what I mean. C'mon."

"Man. Where the fuck is that ambulance? This is ridiculous."

"They're on the way. Busy night, plus I think they had a couple call-offs. It's up to us, man."

"I'm not going in there."

"Well, I'm not going in by myself."

"Someone has to guard the suspect."

"Fuck the suspect. Let's go."

"Who cares if it's eating evidence?" He pointed his gun at Ted. "He already confessed. We're good to go."

Marv shook his head. "Dude, think about it. What do you think Jed's gonna say if he finds out we let some dog munch on one of our DOAs? We'd never hear the end of it."

The other cop paused, considering his options. "Okay. Fuck. *Fuck.* I fuckin' hate dogs."

"C'mon. Help me get this dumbass in my car." Marv kicked Ted again. "Get up, dumbass."

Ted tried to protest, telling them it wasn't like they thought, but one of them elbowed him in the mouth and ordered him to shut the fuck up.

The two cops holstered their weapons and led Ted through the backyard gate, past his own car and to one of the black-and-whites parked in the alley, lights illuminating the pine trees opposite Justin's parents' house. HAMMOND POLICE was painted across the side of the vehicle. Marv opened the back door and they pushed Ted inside then slammed it shut. By the time Ted managed to sit up, the cops were already through the gate, halfway to the house.

"No!" Ted thrashed the side of his head against the window glass. "Don't go in there! You don't understand!"

They either didn't hear him or chose to ignore his

warnings. Probably accustomed to lunatics screaming similar bouts of desperation. One by one they disappeared inside the house, leaving Ted alone. The night became unbearably silent. He rocked like a psych ward patient, trying to convince himself he couldn't hear his own heart beating inside his chest, trying not to think about hearts at all, especially the one he neglected to put a bullet through. This was ridiculous, fucking crazy. The howl didn't mean Justin had been telling the truth. The howl could have been from anything. Maybe the fighter dog never ran away, after all. Only hid somewhere else in the house. A howl didn't mean shit. Werewolves didn't exist. That was horror movie nonsense. Justin had been crazy, pure and simple. There was nothing supernatural about it.

Up front, voices crackled out of the police radio at a low, steady volume. Dispatchers announcing codes that sounded like nonsense. Officers responding with equal incoherency.

Another howl. Much louder and more aggressive than the previous ones. The howl was proceeded by what sounded like a scream, although the rolled-up window made it difficult to tell.

However, the gunshots that followed were unmistakable.

Instinct forced him to lower his head below the window, near his lap, afraid the shot was meant for him. He couldn't stop shaking and crying. Tears and snot splattered against his thigh like raindrops.

More gunshots. More screams.

Another howl.

Jesus Christ, what was *happening* in there?

He used his legs to turn his body sideways and tried opening the back door with his confined hands. Locked, of course. Worth a try.

Another gunshot.

Oh fuck oh fuck.

He turned the other way around and laid on his side, raising his legs to the window and kicking the glass. Nothing happened. He kicked again. Nothing happened. More howling from inside the house, but the gunshots and screams had stopped. *Oh shit.* He kept kicking at the window, but the glass refused to give. It was useless. Cop cars were built specifically so idiots like him couldn't do this very thing.

He sat up, out of breath, and tried to pull his arms apart, hoping the handcuffs around his wrists would magically break. They didn't. He cursed and slammed his shoulder against the door. Did it again. *Again.* The door remained closed. Trapped.

Something appeared at the back door of the house, large and black. Ted stopped moving, hypnotized by the thing prodding out on the porch. It was too dark to fully make out its form. As it neared the gate, the cop car lights managed to reveal more details. Something muscular. *Furry?* Wide, bright eyes. Pointed ears. It walked slowly, on all fours, hunched over like an ape might move, carefully examining its foreign surroundings. Ted remained as still as his nerves would allow, terrified of drawing attention to himself. Refusing to look away. Refusing to blink. Refusing to breathe.

He didn't want the thing to get any closer. He didn't want to see it for what it really was. It wandered the back yard in circles, its head close to the grass. Like a dog sniffing nature, searching for just the right scent to hook its obsession. No goddamn way did that thing just come out of Justin's dead parents' house. No goddamn way was that thing Justin.

"Fuck." Full panic mode now, body shaking and not even realizing it. "This is so fucked."

The thing in the back yard froze, then lifted its head from the grass, toward the cop cars. The siren lights emphasized its face as it stepped closer.

Canine? Yeah. No doubt about it.

But a dog, though?

It wasn't that simple.

The thing approaching the cop car was far more complex than just some *dog*.

It was exactly how Justin had described. Everything he'd said had been the truth. Ted hadn't believed a single word. Even after he shot him in the head. Even after he heard the howls and the screams and the gunshots. He'd still been in denial, told himself other explanations existed, that if he dug hard enough he'd unearth logic for every stream of fear and confusion.

But there was no denying the truth when it was standing five feet away, drool and blood dripping from its massive jaw.

Only the glass of the window separated them now.

The thing's eyes were about the only things that didn't come across as alien. They were familiar. Too familiar.

They belonged to Justin.

"Oh no oh no oh no." Ted tried ripping the handcuffs in half again. No success. Didn't dare redirect his gaze away from the Justin-monster next to the car. It was studying him, almost like his predicament in the back seat was worthy of amusement.

Which was definitely something Justin would have

found hilarious.

God. What a dick.

Ted tried to reason with it. "Please don't. Please please don't. C'mon. It's me. Teddy. We grew up together. We were best friends."—*then you killed my wife and I shot you in the face*—"Please don't do this. Okay? Okay?"

The Justin-monster seemed to consider the request, then let loose a thunderous howl and charged the cop car. Its skull smashed against the door and everything shook. Bone against steel. Ted screamed, which provided further encouragement for the creature to repeat the action, again and again, each time anticipating the charge with a short howl. He could tell the door was denting with each strike, so he scooted to the opposite side of the back seat, lifting his leg up, ready to kick the Justin-monster in the face as soon as it broke through the barricade.

As if sensing Ted's strategy, the Justin-monster turned and hustled to the backyard gate, stopped, one-eightied, howled, and charged again. This time the car didn't just shake. It fucking flipped. The creature's head nailed the door and the two wheels on the passenger's side lifted from the ground. The Justin-monster didn't back away, instead kept pushing, growling and snarling at the steel, then gave it one last push. Ted screamed as the car landed on its roof and gravity threw him against the ceiling. His neck and back cracked and he was positive something had just snapped, paralyzing him for life. Everything throbbed. The handcuffs had dug deeper into his wrists, drawing blood. He bit his tongue to prevent more noise, tried not to move or do anything that might draw attention to his vulnerability.

Glass crunched outside the car. Something circling the wreckage, slowly, taking its time. *Glass?* Yes. The back window, on the driver's side—the side closest to Ted—it had shattered during the landing. Ted couldn't stop shaking. Like his body no longer belonged to him, repossessed after one too many late fees. The Justin-monster's shadow fell upon the pavement next to the shattered window. The footsteps got louder, more glass on this side, the crunching so unbearable, each step setting off a new alarm inside his nerves. A village of tiny specimens in his brain screaming, "It's coming! For the love of god, it's coming!"

The Justin-monster stopped just outside the shattered window, its large head in full view. Its ears stood straight up, alert. The sniffling ceased. Ted watched, unable to look away, nowhere for him to go even if he did want to flee. He couldn't be more trapped. The creature slowly turned his head toward the shattered window. Blood stained the fur of its muzzle. A slab of gore hung from its jaw. Its familiar eyes made contact with Ted's and the creature's heavy breathing stopped.

For one eternal moment, the two beings stared at each other in perfect silence.

Did it recognize him?

It cocked its head. A dog, confused and curious. The growling returned. Slow, but picking up volume in a hurry. More drool and foam formed at its gums. Its fangs out, ready for the attack.

"Justin. Please. Don't."

His beg for mercy came out raw and pathetic. It was all he had left. A part of him hoped the Justin-monster just got it over with already. Rip his fucking throat out and be done with it.

But the moment was interrupted. Somewhere ahead, on another street branching out from the alley perhaps, someone laughed. Then another someone. People walking, joking around, having a good time, probably a little toasted.

The Justin-monster snapped its attention toward the sound.

"MY DICK IS BIG ENOUGH TO FUCK KING KONG." The man sounded maybe a little more than just toasted. "MY DICK IS BIG ENOUGH TO FUCK GODZILLA."

The creature took off down the alley, forgetting all about its easy target trapped in the cop car.

TWENTY-NINE

T ED WAITED ALL OF FIFTEEN SECONDS BEFORE frantically crawling out of the car. Hands still cuffed behind his back, he had to worm through the window, jagged shards of glass slicing at his arms and stomach. The pain felt distant, as if inflicted upon someone else. Actually standing proved to be a more difficult task than anticipated. He had to leverage his back against the flipped-over cop car and crab-walk until free from gravity's pull, the scattered glass threatening to slide him right back down to the ground should he have made one false step.

Somewhere on the next street over, the man with a dick big enough to fuck a kaiju screamed.

"Yo! What the hell is that? OH HOLY SHIT RUN, RUN, RUN!"

The man's friend also screamed something similar.

Their screams evolved into a pitch more agonizing as the Justin-monster caught up with them.

Ted moved his ass, cursing under his breath, trying desperately not to trip as he hobbled toward his car. Then he stopped and realized just how far his current dilemma stretched.

Couldn't drive a car with his hands handcuffed, could

he? Couldn't do much of any goddamn thing.

The screaming from the street over intensified.

Fuck fuck fuck.

He glanced both ways down the alley and determined either direction guaranteed bad news. Only one place he could think of that could unlock these cuffs, and it was the one goddamn place he never wanted to visit again.

Another howl.

More screaming.

Shit.

Ted hurried from the car through the backyard gate, eyes on the screen door, wide open and hanging from its hinges by miracles and not much else. A trail of blood began—*or ended?*—at the stairway platform and led down the steps, into the basement.

He followed it.

Earlier today, walking down these stairs, he'd noticed how bad the basement smelled. Dirty clothes. Old food. Mold. It had smelled like an animal lived down here. But now, going down again? The odor evolved.

The basement smelled like death.

Like a massacre.

He gagged and swallowed vomit. Blood painted not just the floor but also the walls and some of the ceiling. The first cop was in the living room section of the basement, throat and stomach ripped open. Entrails poured out either side of the hole in his gut, resembling an erupted volcano. A scream was frozen on his now pale face. He had died experiencing the worst pain of his life and he had felt every second of it.

It occurred to Ted that the Justin-monster might have eaten the handcuff key while feasting on the cop. Panic sent him collapsing to his knees and scooting around so his back faced the corpse. He stretched his fingers toward the cop's waist and dived into a mess of gore. A thick wall of a slimy substance tried to suck in his hands, but he persisted, feeling around the cop's belt loop until he recovered an assortment of keys attached to a retractable reel. Relief hit him so hard he started crying.

Next came an even greater challenge: figuring out which key was meant for the cuffs, and how to insert it into the lock—all while his hands were confined behind his back and the dead cop's blood soaked into his ass. The keys, covered in the cop's innards, kept slipping from his grasp. Thoughts of scooping the guts from a pumpkin flashed in his mind and he nearly had to swallow another mouthful of vomit.

Somewhere in the distance, sirens wailed.

Surely heading to 209 Gostlin.

Two officers investigate a reported homicide, then never update their superiors? Yeah. No fucking doubt about it. Backup was on the way, and they weren't messing around. Maybe they *thought* they were fearing the worst, but they had no fucking idea. They would soon enough, and Ted had to be far away before they arrived. He thought he could face the music and own up to everything that had happened, but no, he couldn't have been more wrong. Not after seeing Justin in full wolf mode up close. What the hell was he supposed to say about that? No words would ever convince a single soul. Hell, it hadn't even convinced *him*, not until he'd witnessed it with his own two eyes.

The fifth key he managed to line up with the cuffs slipped inside the lock like Cinderella's foot into her lost shoe. He gasped and twisted it and one of the handcuffs uncurled from his wrist. He brought his arms around and groaned, not realizing how stiff and sore he'd become until stretching. He fumbled for the keys again and quickly unlocked the second cuff. He tried climbing up to his feet and slipped in the blood, falling face-first into the torn-open cop corpse.

The sirens sounded closer now, but Ted still couldn't bring himself to leave the basement. Not until he saw her one last time. Not until he said his goodbyes.

He found the second cop in the bedroom area, in a worse state than the previous one. The Justin-monster had also snacked on the man Ted shot, the enraged father of the boy Justin paid to slaughter stray animals.

The room was a disaster. Any other cops who walked in here would immediately put in their two-weeks' notice. Broken pieces of steel were scattered around the floor, dipped in blood. The chains imprisoning Justin's body must have exploded during his transformation. Jesus Christ, if those couldn't keep him detained, what would?

Unable to stop himself, as if caught in a trance, he opened the deep freezer.

He stared at Shelly and Shelly stared back.

In a series of unintelligible shouts, he apologized and begged for her forgiveness.

And waited for a response that was never going to come.

THIRTY

TED GOT IN HIS CAR AND BACKED OUT BETWEEN the two cop cars—one on its hood, the other still on its wheels—and drove out of the alley. Barely ten seconds passed before half a dozen police vehicles bolted down the boulevard opposite of him and swerved into the gravel trail leading to the back of 209 Gostlin. Ted increased his speed. Nobody was going to pull him over right now. Any available units were far too busy with the clusterfuck back at Justin's parents' house. He gunned it onto I-90 and headed east.

The drive to his mother-in-law's house took less than ten minutes. At this hour, the highway was mostly deserted. He swerved in and out of lanes, exhausted, every ounce of his body in intense pain. He flipped through the radio stations but everything playing was bullshit. Old rock songs about lost loves. New rock songs about lost loves. Talk shows about liberal pussies trying to take away the guns from hard-workin' Americans. Talk shows about hard-workin' Americans shooting liberal pussies for protesting the government. Talk shows about what the president recently tweeted. Commercials about local mattress stores. Commercials about the latest heart attack sandwich offered at McDonald's. It was all just a bunch of goddamn noise. All he wanted to do was sleep, get some rest, forget any of this ever happened. But he couldn't. His night was not yet done.

It never would be.

He parked in front of his mother-in-law's house and cut the engine. He sat there and watched the dark residence, trying to control his breathing, deciding what he was going to say and realizing it didn't matter, that any speech he gave her would end badly. He'd come back to Percy to deliver the news in person, and the only news he had was about the worst bit of news a man could give to someone else.

Ma'am, your daughter was murdered by my best friend. He ripped her head off and ate her body. You see, she caught him at a difficult time in his life.

No matter which way he planned it out in his head, it always went to shit.

He got out of the car. The cul-de-sac was pitch black, not a shimmer of light in the area. A neighborhood like this, nobody stayed awake past midnight. Old folks mostly. People who had long embraced retirement. Shelly's parents had moved in back in the late nineties. Her dad had been in the military until a bullet to the shoulder forced him to call it quits, then he sold discount tires until a heart attack claimed him about five or so years ago. Only Shelly's mom lived there now. Linda. A woman who had once told Ted he would only end up ruining her daughter's life.

Well, she hadn't been wrong.

He twisted the knob and found the front door unlocked. Not a surprise. For one thing, there wasn't a lot of crime on this side of Percy. Most people who lived in this cul-de-sac—and the ones surrounding it—probably didn't bother enabling their locks. And also, Ted assumed Linda had specifically left it unlocked in case Shelly decided to return to her house in the middle of the night and couldn't find the spare key.

He kicked off his shoes in the hallway and followed the sound of a TV playing at a low hum in the living room. Linda snored on the couch, sitting up, head slouched forward. He considered shaking her awake and getting it over with, then realized, given how much like an absolute lunatic he probably looked, there was a good chance she'd start screaming as soon as she laid eyes on him.

The bathroom door tended to creak. Same with the floors. Old house and all that. He took his time closing it, waiting until the final *click* before flipping on the light. One glance in the mirror and he knew he'd made the correct decision delaying his conversation with Linda. Holy shit did he look like hell. Face stained with blood. Both eyes blackened. Nose crooked and bruised. Lips swollen and cut. Scratches ran up and down his flesh like abstract tribal tattoos. Clothes torn up, soaked in not just his own blood but the blood of multiple others.

Jesus Christ, what a hell of a night.

He shed what remained of his attire and discarded it in the trash can next to the toilet, then turned on the shower, stepping in immediately, not giving a shit how cold the water came out. He welcomed its icy chill. Jolted him awake faster than any can of Monster or cup of coffee could ever dream of doing. The temperature soon warmed, then grew so hot his flesh felt like it was on fire, but he did not flinch. He embraced the scalding water like a sinner kneeling before the whip. He deserved this and much,

much more.

It wasn't until he was drying off with one of Linda's sunflower-decorated towels that it occurred to him he didn't have any spare clothes here. And he couldn't very well retrieve the torn-up ones from the trash can, could he? Just touching them again would require another shower. Towel wrapped around his waist, he tiptoed out of the bathroom and down the hall, hoping like hell Linda hadn't woken up yet. He darted straight for Shelly's childhood bedroom, where she'd undoubtedly been sleeping since walking out on him. The sheets were a mess on top of the mattress. He thought about throwing off his towel and collapsing onto the bed and curling up in her blanket and crying against her pillow but if he did that he was liable never to get up again. Save it for later, once he was finished telling Linda all he had to tell. If she called the cops afterward, fine, he could still get more crying done in whatever hole the Percy Police Department locked him up in. A man could cry anywhere if he was ambitious enough.

He found a blue flannel on the floor next to her dresser. It had once belonged to him until Shelly one day claimed it as her new pajamas. There had been no use in protesting, especially when he saw how she looked with it on. The first four buttons unbuttoned, no bra, the pale smoothness of her breasts almost inviting his face to nuzzle between them. No bottoms of any kind besides panties, the flannel ending halfway down her bare thighs. The way the flannel would ride up whenever she bent over, revealing just enough to make him fall completely under her spell.

He'd told her she could keep it, that it was hers, hers forever, but of course he hadn't just been talking about the flannel, no, not really.

Ted closed his eyes and pressed the flannel against his face. It smelled just like her. For a second it was like she was still alive, like she was in the room with him and everything was okay. He slipped it on and hugged himself, tried to squeeze his chest tight enough to make time travel possible. The only thing in the room that even somewhat fit his fat ass were a pair of gray sweatpants with the word "BOO-TY-LICIOUS" across the butt in bright pink bubble letters. He'd bought them for her a few years ago at Walmart for $5, and laughed the whole way home, thinking she'd take one look at them and demand he turn around and ask for a refund. But she ended up loving them, said they were perfect to lounge around the house in.

Blue flannel and booty-licious sweatpants. If it made him feel closer to his wife, then he didn't give a shit how he looked. Who was he trying to impress, anyway?

The bedroom door creaked open. Ted spun around, spotted Linda's head peeking through the crack, no doubt checking to see if her daughter had already fallen asleep. Probably heard him taking a shower and thought it was Shelly, finally home, finally safe. Her gaze traveled from the empty bed to her son-in-law standing next to the dresser. She didn't scream, although her expression certainly looked like she wanted to.

A gasp, then a whisper. "*Ted?*"

He reached out for her, not sure what he intended on doing with his hand, and stepped forward. "Linda, I—"

"What are you *doing* here?" She surveyed the room again. "Where's my daughter?"

"Linda—we...we gotta talk."

THIRTY-ONE

THERE WAS NO SIMPLE WAY TO TELL A MOTHER HER daughter had been slaughtered and eaten by a werewolf. Any way Ted worded it would be wrong. And the longer he tried beating around the bush, the worse she'd react. It was already obvious something terrible had happened. His poker face was pathetic, always had been, and tonight was no different. Plus, if she was okay, why was he here and she wasn't? Where the hell *was she* then?

So he sat her down on the couch and held her hand and told her the truth.

"Linda...Shelly...Shelly's dead."

The color drained from Linda's face. "What? What are you saying?"

"She's dead. I'm sorry, but it's true. She's dead. She was... she was killed."

"*What are you saying?*" Spit flew from her mouth and she squeezed Ted's hand hard enough to make it numb. "*What did you do to my little girl?*"

Ted tried to get away but the old lady's grip was iron-clad. He regretted coming here. What the hell had he been thinking? No way was he qualified to deliver this kind of news. He was the last person she wanted to hear this shit from.

"I didn't do anything!" Even he didn't believe the words as they trickled out of his mouth. "It wasn't me, okay? It wasn't me. I swear to god it wasn't me."

Her grip somehow tightened, like she was trying to rip his hand off at the wrist.

"*What happened?*"

"If you let go of me, I'll tell you, okay? Shit, that's what I'm trying to do, isn't it? I'm trying to tell you what happened."

She didn't let go, didn't loosen her hold. "*What happened?*"

Tears spilled down her eyes but she refused to blink. Her stare chilled his heart. Could she see inside of him? Could she see his secrets, his fears?

"Do you remember my friend—Justin?"

"*What friend?*"

"Justin! The kid we grew up with. The one with the basement."

"*What happened to my daughter, goddamn you?*"

Linda's body shook from head to toe but she did not let go of Ted's wrist. He feared she was on the verge of a heart attack. A terrible part of him prayed it happened, anything to let him leave this house as quickly as possible. Shit, he should have never fucking come here. How goddamn stupid. Jesus Christ.

"Justin, okay? It was Justin. He was sick. He couldn't help it."

Linda leaned forward, murder in her eyes. "What are you talking about?"

"Justin, he was…he was sick. He didn't mean to. Shelly… she went over to his house. She wanted someone to talk to.

And…and he killed her. It was an accident."

"An…*accident?* What are you *saying?* What *is this?*"

"I thought…I thought he was crazy. That he did it on purpose. But I know…I know the truth now. He didn't mean to. He was—he was infected with this…this *disease*, okay? And it made him violent, made him not himself. And she was there when it happened, when he lost control, and she…she *died*."

Linda released her grip and folded her hands in her lap. Her gaze dropped to the floor. The crying took control. "I don't—*I don't understand.* I don't understand what you're saying."

Ted didn't respond, didn't have the right words. How could he make her understand what had happened when he didn't even get it?

She had to know the rest of it.

He kept going.

"He called me earlier today, asked me to come over. He told me about his sickness, then he…he showed me what he had done. To Shelly. Oh…god. I can still see her, Linda. I can still see her."

Linda was crying too hard now to say anything.

"And I lost control. I couldn't…I couldn't process. He had this gun, and I took it from him, and I…and I shot him. I killed him. I killed him for what he did to Shelly. He's dead, Linda. He…he's dead."

There was nothing else to say, and even if there was, Ted wasn't the one to say it. He reached out and tried hugging Linda. She accepted and returned the embrace. Together they sobbed. Tears soaking into each other's shoulders. The 24/7 news station on the TV still playing, undisturbed by their emotional wreckage.

Eventually Linda broke contact and got off the couch. She wandered aimlessly through the living room, touching random photograph frames and table corners. Searching for a purpose that didn't exist. What did a mother do after learning her daughter had been killed? Ted couldn't imagine. Even watching her move around now, he had no goddamn idea, and he didn't think she did either. After a minute or two of circling the same areas, she leaned her back against the wall and slid down to her ass then buried her face in her palms, trying to wipe the tears from her eyes that would never stop coming.

Ted contemplated if enough time had passed for him to leave yet, but felt like if he made any sudden moves she would tear out his throat. Wasn't like he had anywhere else to go, anyway. This house was the closest he'd ever feel to being close to Shelly again. Might as well take advantage of it. After tonight he very much doubted he'd return.

"Oh, Lord." Linda softly thumped the back of her head against the wall. "I need a cup of coffee. What about you?"

Ted nodded. It was exactly what he needed.

The time on his cell phone informed him it was well past one in the morning. Ted felt sure he'd never sleep again. No matter how exhausted he became, him and sleeping were finished. Ex-lovers going their separate ways. No. Bad metaphor. Terrible fucking metaphor. If that was even a metaphor. Ted didn't fucking know. It didn't matter. How could he ever have the balls to rest again, after everything he'd seen? Only a coward would feel comfortable sleeping after discovering his wife's decapitated head in a deep freezer. No. Ted didn't deserve to sleep ever again. Sleep was for the innocent. And Ted was anything but.

Ted sat at the same kitchen table Shelly had eaten dinner

at every night during her childhood. He'd never noticed it before, but it bore a remarkable similarity to the table found in Justin's parents' kitchen. For a bizarre moment Ted felt like he'd never left the Hammond house, that he was still in the kitchen, arguing about McDonald's with Justin. Except the person standing by the coffee pot wasn't his best friend. It was his dead wife's mother. Both her hands on the counter preventing her old, fragile body from crumbling to the linoleum. Back facing Ted. Staring intently at the coffee pot as black liquid resembling motor oil slowly trickled into the carafe. She was still shaking. So was Ted. He hoped the coffee pot never filled and they just stayed like that, watching it fail to complete this impossible task, never having to say another word to each other again. She grabbed two small mugs from the cupboard and filled them to their brims. The way she looked at Ted as she brought them over to the table gave Ted the feeling she would have rather tossed the coffee in his face. He wouldn't have blamed her. He wouldn't have even raised his hand as a shield.

She sat across from him and they took turns sipping their coffees. Eyes burning from excessive crying. Nostrils raw from tissues. Throats restricting. If someone didn't say something soon then it was likely nobody would ever say anything again, which didn't sound so bad to Ted.

Linda sipped her coffee then set the cup down in front of her. "How did he do it?"

"What?" More of a distraction than a real question. He knew exactly what she meant.

"The…the monster who killed my daughter. How did he do it." Also not a real question, but a demand. "Tell me."

"I don't—you don't want to hear this. Please. Trust me."

"It doesn't matter if I want to hear it. I need to."

Ted didn't know how to argue that. Flashes of Shelly's head in the deep freezer. Her eyes lifeless yet somehow still staring up at him.

Vertigo made the kitchen spin 'round and 'round. He closed his eyes and rubbed his temple. Sipped some more coffee. It tasted terrible. He raised the cup back to his lips and drank even more. It still tasted terrible. He kept doing it until Linda snapped her fingers at him and he opened his eyes again, seeing her leaning over the table, her face consisting of something like fear and anger and utter defeat all mixed into one massive shit pie.

"Tell me. Goddamn you. Tell me."

"Well. Like I said. Justin…he was sick."

"Sick with *what?*"

"I'm not sure. The police don't know yet. He got bit by a dog or a wolf or…something. The wound got infected and it made him…get violent, I guess. Lose control, forget where he was, forget *who* he was. He didn't mean what he did to Shelly. He didn't understand what was happening. She came over to his house…to, you know. Talk about me. About the stupid things I'd done to her. And he had one of his…uh…episodes. She got in his way. *He didn't mean to.*"

"You've said that."

"I shot him."

"You've said that, too."

"Oh."

"But you haven't told me what he did to her."

"I don't know all the details."

"Did…did she suffer?" Linda gulped and fresh tears streamed down her cheeks. The question she'd really meant all this time. "Ted? Did she suffer?"

He shook his head. "No. I was told it had been quick.

Painless. She didn't feel a thing."

"He didn't…you know."

"Didn't what?"

"*Rape her.*"

The idea sounded so ridiculous he almost laughed, which itself was a terrifying thought. Only a deranged sociopath could possibly find humor in a night such as this.

"No. He didn't…he didn't *rape* her."

"Okay." She stared into her coffee cup long enough for Ted to wonder if the conversation had finally come to an end. It amazed him how well she was handling the situation. He wondered if she had already known Shelly was dead before he came here tonight. Some kind of mother's intuition. "Why haven't the police called me?"

"What?"

"The police haven't contacted me."

"Why would they?"

"I'm her mother."

"Yeah, and I'm her husband."

Talking in the present tense, like she was still someone's daughter, still someone's wife.

"I'm going to call them. I have to call them. They'll know more about what's going on."

She got up and headed toward the phone connected to the wall. Ted jumped up and cut her off.

"No! You can't."

Paranoia paled her face. "What? Why can't I?"

Ted struggled to spit out an excuse. "Well…it's…it's late, you know? The people, the cops who know about the case…the murder…they're home by now. It'd be better to call tomorrow, in the afternoon maybe."

She didn't seem fazed by this explanation. "I'm not

waiting until tomorrow! My *daughter* has been *killed*, god-dammit! I need answers *now*."

She tried to maneuver around him and he shoved her, rougher than he'd meant.

"I already told you what happened!"

Linda pushed him back and he almost fell. "You're not telling me everything! You're lying! You're not telling me what really happened. Not everything. I don't believe a goddamn word you say."

"I'm not lying to you, Linda. *Please* believe me."

"If you weren't holding anything back, then you wouldn't be trying to stop me from calling the cops."

"No, I—"

"They're probably after you right now, aren't they?" A grim little smile spread across her face. "Of course they are. Do you think I'm some dumb old lady? No! I see exactly what's going on here. What did you do, you lousy no good son of a bitch? *What did you do to my daughter?*"

"Linda, I—"

She turned from him and threw open a drawer next to the sink, then reached in and pulled out a large chef's knife. She held it over her head and the blade's cleanliness winked at him.

"What are you—"

"Get out of my way or I swear to god I'll use it. I don't know what you've done but I'm going to find out, one way or another."

Bullshit. There was no way she'd stab him.

He stepped forward and held out both hands, palms out, a truce. "Linda, please, I promise I—"

Then she stabbed him.

THIRTY-TWO

F OR A MOMENT, TED LIVED IN BLISSFUL DENIAL.
He stared at the knife not with horror but
wonder. Linda had released her grip on the handle
the moment it entered his left hand, and now there it remained. Stuck in his goddamn hand. It'd gone through his
palm and one half of the blade stuck out through the back
of his hand. When he moved his arm, the knife moved with
him, like it was just another limb he'd somehow forgotten
about. Like the skin of his hand had morphed, evolved into
something oblong and sinister.

Blood oozed out of both ends of the hole and poured
down his arm.

Then the pain finally registered.

He screamed. So did Linda, who still stood in front of
him. She looked about as shocked at what she'd done as
he was.

"You fucking stabbed me!"

"I told you to get out of my way!"

She tried stepping around him and he punched her
with his uninjured hand. His fist cracked against her jaw
and she let out a soft *ooof!* then crumpled to the floor.

He kept his hand raised to his face, eyes wide and

mouth wider. No matter how hard he stared at the knife in his hand it refused to disappear.

Linda lay unconscious on the floor, and he hoped like hell he hadn't just killed her. He stepped over her limp body and held his hand over the sink. Blood stained porcelain and escaped down the drain.

"Jesus Christ. Oh fuck."

He wrapped his fingers around the knife's handle and tried to pull. The goddamn thing wouldn't budge. He screamed and hunched over the sink. It was stuck in there good. Just touching the handle seemed to increase the blood flow. *Fuck fuck fuck.* Surely a man couldn't walk around with a knife sticking through his hand. Not only would infection eventually spread, but it was just impractical on every level of human functioning. No. He had to get it out.

"Goddammit."

He grabbed a sponge from the dish drainer and stuffed it in his mouth. He bit down. It tasted exactly how he expected: like a sponge.

This time when he grabbed the handle, he didn't bother trying to pull the knife. Instead he gripped the handle until his knuckles whitened then yanked his other arm hard and fast.

The edge of the chef's knife widened the hole with every millimeter of progress. He didn't stop until the blade slipped free. His grasp loosened and the knife bounced off the porcelain. Blood streamed out of the hole in his hand like a busted dam. It fucking geysered.

Ted screamed hard enough to rip his lungs in half. His uninjured hand searched frantically for something to wrap around the wound, coming upon a dirty washcloth thrown across the dish drainer. He pressed it to his palm. Not long enough to wrap around his hand but at least it was something. Blood instantly soaked through it and rendered the item useless. Arm tucked against his stomach, he stumbled through the kitchen, nearly tripping over his mother-in-law. *Ex*-mother-in-law.

He discarded the washcloth and held his hand under the bathroom sink faucet as he searched the cabinets below for gauze. Some old hair dye. A bottle of peroxide. Small cartoon band aids that wouldn't have done shit for his wound. The water continued washing through his hand, turning pink as it poured out the opposite end.

No way in hell could he go to a hospital. By now, the police surely had his name in their database. It wouldn't have taken long to track down his information, given he'd used his own cell phone to confess to murder. Sooner or later they'd find him. And who cared if they did? Not like he had much to live for at this point. His life was ruined, as far as he saw it. No future awaited him. No future he desired, anyhow.

Fuck. What a day.

What a goddamn day.

He took a towel hanging next to the sink and wrapped it around his hand, tightening it in place with a knot. The front of his blue flannel had darkened with blood. His booty-licious sweatpants, however, remained clean.

Back in the kitchen, he found Linda standing next to the sink, one hand rubbing her already bruising jaw, the other holding the chef's knife. Blood dripped from the blade. She pointed it at him, but the fight he'd once seen in her eyes had disappeared.

Ted slapped the knife out of her hand and it flew across

the kitchen.

He pointed at the table. "Sit down and I'll tell you what happened. What really happened."

In the freezer above the fridge he dug out a bag of frozen vegetables, which he tossed on the table.

"For your face."

She understood and pressed the bag against her jaw. He didn't know what good it would actually do, but that's what characters in movies always did, so he figured it wouldn't hurt to give it a shot.

He took their coffee mugs and dumped out the cold liquid then refilled them. He gave one to her and sipped from his own. Somehow it tasted less terrible now. Maybe his body was in too much shock to find offense with a beverage.

He sat across from her and stared at his hand a long while before speaking. The towel was wet with blood but it still had a lot more it could absorb before a new one would be necessary. He wondered how much it could possibly bleed. Surely soon enough it would stop. Either that or he'd pass out. He tried to bend his fingers and found the task impossible. She'd gotten him good.

"Okay." He sighed. Linda sat, watching, waiting. "You want to know what really happened tonight? I'll tell you. But fair warning: you're not going to believe me."

And he told her.

He told her everything.

And after they both finished crying, Linda asked only one question.

"What now?"

Ted told her he didn't know, but wished like hell he did.

THIRTY-THREE

As LINDA REFILLED THEIR COFFEE MUGS, TED'S phone dinged in his pocket. He took it out and read the notification. An emergency alert from his Northern Indiana news app:

ALERT!!! HAMMOND RESIDENTS! ALERT!!!
Possible bear loose near HERMIT PARK. Multiple
injuries. Unknown fatalities. Police urge to stay inside. DO
NOT APPROACH ANIMAL.

He stared at the notification awhile, not saying a word, heartbeat out of control. Everything was forgotten, including the throbbing hole in his hand. He read the notification over and over, as if some magic answer would unlock if he looked at it enough times.

"That's him, isn't it?" Linda's voice cracked over his shoulder. Ted jumped and dropped his phone on the table. It bounced against the wood with the strength of an exclamation mark.

He turned around, unsure when she'd snuck up behind him. "What?"

She pointed at the phone. "The bear. They're talking

about your friend, right? The man who…"

He considered lying, then realized he had no reason not to tell the truth. "Yeah." He nodded and picked up the phone again. "I think so."

Wasn't no *think* about it. Not really.

Of course it was Justin. How could it possibly be anybody else? On the hunt again. On another killing spree. This time, someone had seen him, someone who survived to tell the tale. This time the police were after him. They knew what he looked like. But how much did they *really* know? Did they actually think they were only dealing with a bear? What would they do once they finally apprehended the creature? Something told Ted their bullets weren't gonna do shit. Not unless they were made out of silver.

"They're not going to be able to stop him, are they?"

He shook his head. "I don't think so. I don't know. Maybe."

"He's going to kill a lot more people tonight, isn't he?"

"Yeah."

"Well, what are you going to do about it then?" She talked to him like she was speaking to a child, which was not entirely inaccurate.

"What do you mean?"

Linda sighed and the bags below her eyes darkened. "You said so yourself, Ted. It's your fault he got away. Which means it's also your fault that these people are getting hurt. If you'd done what he had asked you to do, then nobody else would have died tonight."

"I—"

She held up her hand. "No. I'm talking."

He shut up.

"You're the only person who knows what is really going

on, which makes you the only person capable of possibly stopping him. This is your responsibility." She paused a beat. "After what you let happen to my daughter, this is the very *least* you could do."

Ted felt another crying fit coming on, but took a couple deep breaths and buried the tears back where they belonged. "I don't know how to stop him."

"Yes you do."

"Unless you have some silver bullets stashed away, I'm out of ideas."

Linda contemplated the situation, then gestured to the archway leading to the dining room. "No silver bullets, but I might have something else that could work."

Ted hesitated, then followed her out of the kitchen. He still wasn't completely sure his mother-in-law believed him. She could be leading him into a trap. What kind of trap could an elderly woman such as her have waiting for him, he didn't know, but it did him no good to move about without his guard up. She had accepted his werewolf yarn with little convincing. Could she have been buying time before coming up with a new plan to stab his other hand, or was she so desperate for an explanation she'd acknowledge any form of reality, no matter how bizarre and fantastical?

In the dining room, Linda stopped in front of a china cabinet and opened one of the doors. She pulled out a small display of spoons, forks, and dinner knives. Nothing sharp enough to do any real damage. Ted relaxed, but only slightly.

"My mother gave these to me many, many years ago." She smiled at the memory. "I had always intended to give them to Shelly on her wedding day, but then…when the time came, I couldn't do it. I wanted to keep them. It was selfish, but I don't care. I'm old. I'm allowed to be selfish about things."

Ted shuffled his feet, unsure why she was showing him this. Perhaps some form of dementia had begun eating away at her brain, or maybe she was simply searching for a distraction. "Uh, cool. Those are nice."

She pushed the display toward Ted. "Take them."

"What? I don't want them." He backed away.

"Ted. They're made out of silver. Real silver."

He stopped and inspected the display again. "Oh." He thought about it some more. "Wait, what am I supposed to do with these?" Justin would rip his head off before he ever managed to somehow slip one of those forks inside his heart. Wasn't no way in hell. He doubted one of those knives could even cut through a steak, must less a werewolf's sternum.

But she kept pushing the display at him until he accepted it. He tried to take them from her with both hands, but as soon as he tried curling his left hand around the handle he cried out in pain and bent over. The display of silverware crashed to the carpet. Linda screamed, although less from pain and more from shock, and kneeled to recover the scattered items. Ted hurried back into the kitchen, no real goal in mind, only to keep moving. The pain tended to worsen while stationary. Bending his fingers to grab the silverware display had only succeeded in making his wound more excited. A new wave of blood gushed out of the hole and soaked through his towel. He unwrapped the ruined fabric and dropped it in the sink and held his hand under the cold water streaming from the faucet.

Linda stomped after him, the silverware now safety back in its display and hugged against her chest. "Do you have any idea what these are worth?"

Ted ignored the question. "What about the guns?"

"*What* guns?"

"Didn't your husband—you know, before he passed—didn't he have a gun cabinet or whatever in his office? Are they still there?"

She set the silverware display down on the table and shook her head. "I sold them all a few years ago. What use does an old lady like myself have with a bunch of rifles?"

"You *sold* them?"

"Funerals aren't cheap." Her voice cracked. "You'll come to learn this soon enough."

His phone dinged again from the table. "Can you check that? This won't stop bleeding."

Linda leaned over the phone and squinted. "The *bear* is still on the loose. Five official deaths—oh, Lord—three of them police officers. Over a dozen others severely injured. Ted, you have to stop him. Now, before anyone else dies. This has gone on long enough."

Ted gritted his teeth. Veins pulsated down his wrist. "Get me another towel."

Both hands on her hips, head cocked. "Please."

"*Please.*"

She returned from the bathroom with a couple hand towels and a first aid kit. Where the hell had she found one of those, anyway? He'd searched everywhere in that bathroom and came up empty. Nothing in there would be of much use if he couldn't get the bleeding to stop. Nausea threatened to render him unconscious. A balloon inside his head acquired a leak and farted out air. Goddamn he was tired. When had been the last time he slept? Days. Months. Years. After so long, there wasn't much difference.

He pointed at the stove. "Turn on one of the burners.

One of the big ones." A beat. "Please."

"Wh–why?"

"Because if I bleed any more, I'm gonna fuckin' die."

"But what does that—?"

"Will you please just turn on the stove?"

She approached the oven and stopped, examining the knobs. "What temperature?"

"On HIGH. Turn it…turn it all the way."

"What are you ma—"

"Please just do it. Trust me."

Ted found an alcohol wipe in the first aid kit and ripped it open with his teeth, then tried his best to rub both sides of his wounded hand. Upon first contact with the wipe he released one hell of a scream. Stung like a motherfucker, but he didn't stop until the wipe was too bloody to accomplish anything else.

"Fuck it."

He stomped across the kitchen toward the oven. It was an electric one, so no actual flames spat out. The burner had evolved to a bright, terrifying red.

Linda stood next to him, visibly afraid. "What are you going to do?"

Ted sighed. "Something…stupid."

He'd seen countless movies and TV shows that involved people cauterizing wounds. Every single time it looked painful as hell. Did it actually work? He had no idea. He wasn't a doctor. But he was out of options. Either wrap it up with another towel and pray the bleeding stopped by itself, or *do* something about it.

Ted was going to do something about it.

The urge to punch his mother-in-law in the face again returned.

He grabbed a wooden spoon from the counter and stuck it in his mouth and bit down.

Fingers spread wide, he pressed his palm against the burner.

Fuck fuck fuck fuck—

"—FUCK FUCK FUCK FUCK FUCK—"

The spoon spat out of his mouth.

Somewhere far, far away Linda shouted at him that he was crazy.

He lasted maybe five seconds before the pain got the better of him and he flipped his hand around and pressed the back of it against the burner.

He couldn't have said how long he lasted on the second round. His eyes blinked and when they opened, he found himself sprawled out across the kitchen floor. The scent of burning flesh fresh in the air.

Linda stood above him, hands at her swollen jaw, eyes wide. If she was so concerned about his health maybe she shouldn't have fucking stabbed him. That's what he wanted to tell her, at least. And maybe if he'd been stronger, he actually would have. Instead he slowly sat up and examined his hand. Both sides of his limb now hosted disgusting scabs. It reminded him of pics he'd once seen on the internet of people stricken with leprosy. He grabbed the edge of the sink with his uninjured hand and boosted himself up to his feet. Linda still hadn't said anything. He stepped around her and turned off the oven. Flecks of charcoaled skin hung from the burner.

"How long was I out?" When she didn't respond, he turned back around and cleared his throat. "Huh?"

"I don't know. Not long. Maybe thirty seconds."

"Do you have any pain killers?"

"I...I think there's some Vicodin in the bathroom. From when I had my gallbladder removed."

"Go get 'em."

While she disappeared, he ran cold water from the sink over his hand again, then ripped open a triple antibiotic wipe and attempted to clean his double-sided wound. The sting proved too intense and he dropped the wipe almost immediately. Fuck it. The first aid kit was equipped with bandages of various sizes, including ones about the size of his palm. He took out two of them and applied where necessary.

Linda returned to the kitchen shaking a white bottle and frowning. "There's only a couple left, I think."

Ted took the bottle from her without responding and dumped out the last two pills on the counter. He tossed them both in his mouth without a second thought then leaned over the sink and washed them down with the water pouring from the faucet.

Linda cleared her throat behind him. "I may have sold all of Arthur's weapons, but that doesn't mean I sold *mine*."

Slowly realizing what she meant, Ted turned around and found Linda next to the kitchen table, a shotgun dangling at her side.

"Whoa."

"You think this might be of some help?"

"I don't know. I suppose it wouldn't hurt. Give it to me."

Linda laughed. "You ever operate one of these before?" Her amusement died and was replaced by a sudden darkness, and Ted understood why: there was no greater sin than finding humor in the night you learn your child's been murdered.

Ted shook his head. "I'm sure I can figure it out."

"With your hand being the way it is?"

"Hey, you're the one who—"

Linda nodded. "And I would do it again without any hesitation."

"Thanks."

She gestured toward the living room, toward the front door. "C'mon. Let's go."

Ted bit his tongue. "Let's?"

"Well, someone has to be around to shoot the son of a bitch who killed my daughter, don't they?"

He glanced again at his hand and grimaced. "You sure you want to do this?"

Linda sighed, like he was patronizing her or something. She aimed the shotgun at the silverware on the table. "Your other hand work good enough to pick these up?"

"I think so."

"Then come on. We're taking my car."

THIRTY-FOUR

TED DIDN'T ARGUE. HELL, HE PREFERRED SHE DROVE. It gave him some time to shut his eyes for a little bit. They were so goddamn heavy he couldn't stand it. Sleep hadn't been intended, but that's exactly what happened the moment he sat down in the passenger's seat of Linda's 1990 Chrysler. How that old piece of junk still ran, the universe would never know.

He blinked and discovered he'd somehow been transported from his mother-in-law's house in Percy to the front of Justin's parents' house in Hammond.

One look at the place erased all thoughts of more sleep. He jolted forward, drenched in sweat, and swallowed back a scream. The pain in his hand had somehow gotten worse during his brief nap. He had never expected to see this house again, not in this lifetime at least. But here they were, not even three hours after his last visit. The front of the house was dark and undisturbed. Most nights, that wouldn't have been unusual, but on this particular night it didn't make a lot of sense, considering everything that'd gone down in the basement. The place should have been decorated with police caution tape and illuminated with flashing red and blue lights. The way it looked now, nobody would ever believe such an insane series of slayings had occurred here.

"I think this is the place." Linda cut off the engine. "I only picked up Shelly from here a couple times. So many years ago. But I think this is it."

"It is."

"Shouldn't there be…I don't know. Police cars?"

"Maybe they all went home."

She swallowed and turned from the house, squinting down either side of the street. "Or maybe they're distracted with something else."

"Could be." Ted nodded and the world got dizzier. The old woman read his thoughts exactly. What was more important, a pile of corpses or the monster responsible for them? "They might be around back. Drive to the alley, see if anyone's there."

The cop cars hadn't budged from their positions, one in the gravel driveway, the other flipped over in the alley. If backup had indeed arrived, they didn't seem to give a shit about turning off their dead coworkers' vehicles.

One glance at the ripped-open backdoor made Ted want to vomit. "What are we doing here?"

"I have to see."

"You sure about that?"

"Are you saying you wouldn't go in there, if our positions were reversed?"

Ted gave it some consideration and determined he had no goddamn idea what he'd want to do. Instead he nodded. "I'm not going in again, though. You're on your own."

Linda sighed and sat for a moment, as if working up the guts to get it over with, then she got out of the car and strode through the back yard, shotgun gripped with both hands. Ted leaned his head against the rest and tried to visualize the basement again, the way he'd seen it while retrieving the handcuff keys. That's what his mother-in-law found herself walking into now. And he'd just let it happen, didn't even try to stop her. Lady was liable to suffer from a heart attack the moment she opened the deep freezer. For fuck's sake, that was her *daughter* in there.

He wrapped his good hand around the door handle and tried to pull it open. Nothing happened. He tried again. Still nothing. The soft hum of the car's engine sounded like it was laughing at him. Of course the car was still locked. He gave up and laid his hand back in his lap, having spent all of his energy on the first two attempts to open it. The two Vics he'd popped back at his mother-in-law's house hadn't been as weak as he'd anticipated. A nice numbness branched through his body. He closed his eyes, telling himself he just needed a couple more minutes, that's it, then he'd go inside and console the mother of his dead wife. He'd apologize again and again and beg for forgiveness he knew damn well he didn't deserve and knew she wouldn't give, anyway, and he'd keep on doing it until she got wise and turned that shotgun of hers on him and pulled that definite, merciful trigger.

The driver's door slamming shut woke him up.

Linda behind the wheel again, shaking like she'd fallen prey to hypothermia. Pale enough to camouflage the moon. Ted reached out with his bandaged hand to comfort her and she pushed it away. Instant pain. He screamed.

She put the car in reverse and started backing down the alley, out onto the boulevard. "Where's the park?"

"Where's the what?" He bit his lip, praying the pain away.

"Your phone said the…the *thing* was seen at some park.

How do I get to it?"

"Oh. The baseball fields. Yeah." He pointed left. "Follow that street a couple blocks. Turn left on…uh…one-forty-second." He scratched his head with his good hand and a snowfall's worth of dandruff sprinkled from his scalp. "I think."

Linda stomped on the gas and gunned it down the street. Ted grabbed the support handle on the ceiling above the window. Panic sent jolts of electricity through his veins. The Vicodin high threatened to fade. Not good. If the pills' effects expired, then he had no idea how the fuck he'd be capable of doing anything. He might be better off amputating the whole goddamn hand. Not a chance he'd mention this to Linda, who probably would have been first in line to volunteer. None of it would matter much, anyway, if she kept driving like she'd just robbed a bank. He hoped she drove faster.

He saw the 142nd sign before she did. "Here! Turn left! Now!"

Damn near nailed a car passing the opposite direction. Tires squealed against concrete and howled in the night. Not the kind of howl they were hunting for, though. But they were getting closer.

A few blocks ahead, red and blue emergency lights lit up Hermit Park.

At least a dozen cop cars abandoned along the street and inside the parking lot. Engines still roaring like their drivers had all just stepped out to pick up a pack of smokes. Linda drove past them like she didn't even noticed they existed, and maybe she didn't. The determination on her face was impenetrable. Here was a woman who had come on a mission. Here was a mother who had come to avenge her daughter's killing.

His wife's killing.

Hermit Park consisted of three minor league fields, one full-sized field, and one tee-ball field. A small playground was built next to the tee-ball field and two public rest areas could be found on either side of the property. Linda maneuvered around the empty cop cars and through the parking lot laid out just beyond the outfield fence of one of the minor league fields. If not for the silent emergency lights still going off atop each car, the entire park would be a cloud of darkness. The stadium lights spread throughout the fields failed to offer any additional guidance. They rolled through the parking lot at a snail's pace, Linda hunched forward, head sticking up over the wheel.

Ted peeked out the passenger's window. Dark stains trailed in random directions throughout the parking lot. *Blood?*

"What's the plan?" He felt like an idiot, hoping this elderly woman took the lead, but the thought of confronting the Justin-monster terrified him. Maybe she had a better idea. "What are we going to do?"

She patted the shotgun between them. "We're going to kill him."

"But it's not—"

"We brought silver." She nodded, annoyed, only half-paying attention, her gaze glued on the empty cop cars and the darkness surrounding them. "Once we get him weak enough, we'll take a handful of the silverware and shove it down his fucking throat, if that's what it takes. First we have to—"

"Wait." A thought arrived, eons overdue. "Where are all the cops?"

Linda hit the brakes and pointed ahead. "Over there."

"What?" Ted leaned over the dashboard and squinted toward one of the baseball fields. The headlights only stretched halfway through the outfield before fading into oblivion. He didn't see a damn thing. "Where…?"

Linda sighed and flipped on her brights, illuminating the infield.

Illuminating the cops.

Or, what was left of the cops.

Someone had dragged their bodies onto the pitcher's mound and piled them up like a mountain of death.

No, not someone.

Some*thing*.

The same something currently hunched over the collection of corpses, digging through the bloody remains with its teeth.

Justin.

Ted forgot how to breathe. If he could talk, he would have begged his mother-in-law to turn back, would have convinced her they were making a mistake, that they needed more time to plan this out. But all he could do was sit there in the passenger's seat, his good hand clutching his knee while his bad hand attempted to hide against his stomach.

Rubber squeaked as Linda's fingers tightened around the steering wheel. She released her foot from the brake and stomped on the gas pedal. The car shot forward, throwing Ted's head back against the rest. A wet, desperate shout escaped his lungs, but it was far too late. The car smashed through the outfield fence without so much as a hint of resistance.

The Justin-monster snapped its head over its shoulder and snarled at the approaching target. Linda didn't seem to give a shit that they were driving—at full speed—directly toward a pile of dead policemen. The look on her face made it seem like she would have preferred nothing else—except, perhaps, to hold her sweet daughter in her arms one last time, still full of life, still happy, still hopeful for the future. But that was long out of the cards, so this would have to do, it was all she had, and it was all Ted had, too, whether he'd admit it or not, goddammit, he wanted her to plow right into the mountain of death ahead, wanted her to never take her foot off the gas again.

The Justin-monster abandoned its meal and turned its full body toward them. In the glow of Linda's high beams, it seemed enormous, a proper behemoth fit to destroy many tiny villages. Absolutely *not* the kind of beast two sleep-deprived, widowed lunatics had any right taking on by themselves.

The Justin-monster stretched out on its two hind legs, making itself as tall as possible, and let loose with one tremendous, scary-as-balls howl.

Linda didn't even flinch.

But Ted did.

He squeezed his eyes shut half a second before impact. What followed: a sudden, violent earthquake; the cracking of glass; something heavy rolling into short thuds across the car's roof; the strain of an engine trying to make sense of reality; brakes squealing against grass; something smacking against the front of the car and stopping it in its place.

Ted waited a little while longer before finding the courage to open his eyes again. The corpse of a slaughtered cop rested on top of the hood, staring at Ted with lifeless eyes through the windshield's webbed glass. Half his face was missing. Beyond him, the high beams emphasized more bodies, all similarly brutalized.

The dome light clicked on inside the car, followed by a soft, annoying alarm informing Ted someone had opened the driver's door. A delayed realization: Linda was no longer sitting behind the wheel. Gone, both her and the shotgun. One glance at the rearview mirror confirmed her location. That crazy old bitch. She was really doing it.

Ted scrambled out of the car, shaking, terrified, exhausted. Linda strode toward the Justin-monster kneeling in the grass. No headlights on this side of the car, the darkness more present here, but not enough to hide the shotgun in her grasp. The Justin-monster didn't acknowledge their approach, anyway. The crash had dazed it, maybe, knocked its senses off kilter. Its breaths came out as loud, irregular rasps. Most cars swerved around giant scary monsters. It'd never expected one to come gunning for it.

Linda stopped a foot or two away from the thing that killed her daughter. Fearless.

Ted stopped much farther away. The opposite of fearless. Scared shitless.

He wondered if he should have brought the silverware from the car.

Then the shotgun exploded and the Justin-monster flew to the ground. It slid against the grass then came to a halt.

For one insane moment, the night was silent and still. Both of them frozen in place, watching the creature, waiting for it to make its move. Now was the time to retrieve the silverware and start stabbing the monster's heart with ridiculously expensive knives and forks. But he couldn't bring himself to look away. There it was, limp as the cop corpses on the pitcher's mound. In full wolf mode. The person he'd grown up with. His childhood best friend. His wife's murderer. Blown away by his mother-in-law's shot-gun. Just like that. Done.

The night's silence did not last as long as Ted had hoped.

First, the sound of sirens in the distance, nearing the park. Whoever else still worked for the Hammond Police Department, surely, and probably the neighboring towns, too.

Then, a loud, desperate howl, and the Justin-monster writhed in the grass, an animal in obvious pain. The shotgun went off again and the creature yelped, flipping over on its stomach. A ringing drowned out Ted's ears. The shotgun blasts weren't fucking around. Linda fired again but this time the Justin-monster didn't react. A miss.

"Fuck!" Linda moved closer, making a better effort to aim her weapon.

Ted realized what was about to happen just before it did.

The shotgun went off again as the Justin-monster tackled her. If the blast connected with its target, the creature didn't seem too concerned. The shotgun flew away, discarded somewhere in the darkness.

Linda screamed as the thing's claws slashed across her chest.

Ted sprinted forward, moving on autopilot. He tried to push the Justin-monster off his mother-in-law and it barely moved. It struck out a claw and shoved Ted hard enough to cast him off his feet. God! Such strength! He landed on his ass with a thud but didn't hesitate, climbed right back up and charged again, then immediately stopped at the sight of his mother-in-law's intestines dangling from the Justin-monster's mouth.

Down on the ground, he noticed her throat had been ripped open, too.

"Oh, fuck."

Ted spun around and darted back toward the car, shouting, "OH FUCK OH FUCK OH FUCK," over and over. He should have never fucking come back here. Jesus goddamn Christ how had he ever thought this had been a good idea? He could hear the Justin-monster behind him, right on his trail, inches from reaching out and scooping him up. He dived behind the wheel of Linda's car and slammed the door shut just as the creature smashed against the steel. The wheels on the left side of the vehicle momentarily lifted off the ground. Not enough force to flip the car, but with enough determination it could be easily achievable. Hell, it'd done it before.

Ted wasn't gonna stick around to see it play out that way again.

He pulled the gear shift down to REVERSE and backed away from the mountain of dead policemen. Something scraped against metal and he glanced out the window to find the Justin-monster clawing at his door. Fuck this. He put the car back in DRIVE and floored it the hell out of there.

The Chrysler's engine started sputtering. It was very much a "you have just plowed into a werewolf and will therefore be experiencing slight difficulties using your automobile in the future" sound. He ignored it and drove faster. The claw-scraping stopped. In the rearview the Justin-monster continued giving chase. It would probably never give up until it caught its prey. Until it caught Ted.

He wondered if he had enough gas to make it until sunrise.

He wondered if he even had a choice.

He gunned it through the hole in the outfield fence and skidded through the parking lot, barely dodging all of the abandoned cop cars. Something heavy smashed against steel and he glanced in the rearview just in time to witness the Justin-monster rolling over one of the parked cars, knocking off the emergency lights and tumbling to the pavement.

He made a few quick sudden turns, then straightened out on Dearborn Avenue. No real destination in mind except to get as far away from here as possible.

A couple blocks down, something landed on the back of the Chrysler.

Justin.

Or what had once been Justin.

Jesus fuck. How was it so fast?

He risked a look in the rearview. The goddamn thing had somehow flung half its body onto the trunk. Ted's speed started to decrease. He pressed harder on the gas. Zipping past stop signs like they were mirages, dragging a goddamn werewolf with the back of his car. No, not his car. His mother-in-law's car. His dead mother-in-law. A dead mother-in-law for a dead wife. Everybody was dying but him when he was the one most worthy of death. Except maybe Justin. That goddamn motherfucker.

Red lights blinked up ahead.

Not a stop light.

Train tracks.

"Oh shit oh shit oh shit."

Too late to slow down and turn on another street. He'd just crash into somebody's house. And he couldn't stop and wait for the train to pass. The Justin-monster would rip him out of the window within seconds.

No time to think about it.

GO GO GO.

The tracks were lit up bright. Headlights from a train

way closer than he would have preferred. Fuck it.

The Chrysler smashed through the guard post.

Practically soared over the tracks, he was going so fast.

Already halfway across. He was going to make it. Holy shit. He couldn't fucking believe it.

Then something very fast and very strong exploded against the back of the car and everything was pain and confusion.

THIRTY-FIVE

T ED WOKE UP INSIDE THE CHRYSLER CONVINCED his neck was broken.

Somehow the car had gotten knocked upside down. But how? He reached up at his hip to unbuckle his seatbelt, but it'd never been connected in the first place, which explained why his face was pressed against the glass and his neck was bent at such a stupid angle. Instead he pushed the driver's door open and crawled out.

Two flipped cars in one night. What a world.

A small field of grass next to the street. Vision blurry. Everything spinning. The train was gone but he could still hear it roaring somewhere off in the distance. He got up and surveyed the damage.

"Oh my god."

When he talked, blood spat out of his mouth.

He hardly noticed it, given the state of the scene before him.

The back half of Linda's Chrysler was totaled. Fucking annihilated. Bits and pieces of it were scattered throughout the grass, along with shards of glass and random silver-ware. Blood stained the outside of the car. Not Ted's, even though he was bleeding plenty. Couldn't have been his.

Not up here, on the roof.

Justin's blood.

The train.

It'd smashed straight into him.

Popped him like a zit.

Him or *it,* Ted couldn't decide which was more appropriate.

Him.

Despite all the fucked-up shit Justin had done while wolfed out, that didn't mean he still wasn't human, somewhere, deep down. That didn't mean they still weren't friends. Justin hadn't been the one to kill his wife, his mother-in-law, and everybody else. Not really. Whatever this disease pumping through his blood was, that was the real culprit.

Justin was innocent.

Well, okay, yeah, he'd still decided to get involved with dog fighting, but that didn't mean he was guilty of murdering dozens and dozens of people.

Whoever had sold Justin that fucking hellhound on Craigslist, now *he* was responsible.

He was responsible for all of this.

For Shelly. For Linda. For everybody.

Standing in front of the wrecked car, looking at his best friend's blood, aching from head-to-toe, Ted promised himself he would make it his duty to track this guy down. Surely Craigslist offered some kind of archival files for their members. Or, at the very least, maybe the gas station Justin met him at had been equipped with security cameras. One way or another, he would find him. Then, he would kill him.

Unless, of course, Justin had made the whole Craigslist

encounter up, and something else had turned him into a werewolf. That was always a possibility, especially if the real reason was particularly embarrassing.

The sound of a dying animal broke his concentration.

The sound of Justin.

Howling.

Howling at what, who the hell knew. The moon, the train that had crushed him, maybe howling at Ted. Howling at nothing and howling at everything all at once.

Howling.

He picked up a fork from the ground and took off at a fast limp toward the sound. Time dissolved under the cover of darkness. Justin felt inches away yet at the same time miles apart. Ted continued toward the sound, determined to reach him, no matter the cost.

Then: a large shadow writhing amongst darkness.

The closer Ted got, the clearer Justin became.

Bones poked out of his fur. Half his skull looked caved in. Only one of his eyes remained intact. It was a miracle he was even still breathing.

A miracle or, more likely, a curse.

"Oh, Justin."

Gone, momentarily, was the fear of possibly being mauled to death. Ted kneeled next to his old friend and rested a hand on his shoulder. The bad hand, the one Linda had driven a knife through. Justin moaned softly, looking up with puzzlement. How much was he aware of right now? Did he understand where he was, what he had done? Did he understand that he was dying?

Dying like he'd wanted all night.

That's all he had asked for.

To get it over with.

One silver bullet through the heart.

And Ted couldn't do it. Even when he did want to kill him, he still managed to fuck everything up. Now look at what had happened. *Look*.

"Justin…I'm so sorry…I should have listened be—"

Justin snapped his jaw to the side and bit down on Ted's bandaged hand.

It took him a moment to feel the pain, to realize what was happening.

But when he did, he screamed. Oh yes, he screamed. And if Justin had still been the same "Justin" Ted had grown up with, he would have undoubtedly described Ted's screaming similar to that of a little bitch's.

But instead, Justin only bit down harder.

And Ted screamed louder.

Then he raised his other arm and brought down the silver fork directly into the werewolf's remaining eyeball.

A squeal powerful enough to stop a war and start a thousand more.

Justin ripped his mouth from Ted's hand and slapped him aside like a gnat. Ted flew across the field and knocked his head against a train track still hot from the previous locomotive. All the energy in his body drained at once. He could have easily closed his eyes and fallen asleep then. Never had a more perfect idea ever existed. Maybe he'd get lucky and another train would come plowing through, end this bullshit once and for all.

Somewhere in the darkness, Justin continued announcing his agony to all of Hammond, Indiana.

Ted sat up from the train tracks just in time to notice a large black shadow disappear behind a tree, followed by the triggering of a house's security light.

And against his better judgment, Ted followed.

The security light revealed the severity of his hand's injuries.

It looked worse than he'd anticipated.

It looked a lot fucking worse.

Like a piece of chewed-up meat.

Jesus Christ.

A screen door creaked open and a tall man in his underwear stepped out on the porch, leveling an aluminum baseball bat over his shoulder. "What the fuck you think you're doin'? You wanna get fucked up?"

Ted held up his hand, blood pouring down his arm, as if that was enough of an answer.

The man dropped the bat and it bounced off one of the wooden panels, then rolled toward the end of the porch. "Oh my god. Don't move, I'll call for an ambulance. Holy shit."

He ran back into his house.

Ted scooped up the abandoned baseball bat from the porch and continued on his way. Sirens blasted throughout the night like they were just another part of nature. Ted stumbled through the easement between houses, the bat held loosely in his good hand, dragging the top of it along the grass behind him. Whatever strength remained in his system needed preservation until it became absolutely critical to use up the rest of it.

How much goddamn blood did he have in his body, anyway.

Too fucking much apparently.

He nearly tripped stepping off the curb. Back on the street again. Another street. He couldn't remember which one. No. That wasn't true. Of course he recognized the street.

It was Gostlin.

'Round and 'round the universe spun.

Back, back to Gostlin.

A couple blocks to his right: Justin's parents' house.

Directly to his left: glass breaking, followed by someone screaming.

An alarm went off.

Ted headed left, toward the corner of the intersection. A Mobil gas station, partnered with an On the Run convenience store.

On the Run.

He tried to laugh but only succeeded in spitting out something wet and syrupy. His mouth tasted like pennies. An invisible force squeezed his brain, narrowing his vision.

He couldn't decide if the sirens were getting closer or farther away.

The interior lights of the On the Run were turned off. Closed at midnight, if he remembered right. But the gas pumps remained operational twenty-four-seven. Only a single vehicle was in the lot, a white pick-up in the process of filling up. Ted found the driver hiding in the bed of the truck, pale and trembling.

"You good?"

The driver nodded and pointed at the store. "Some fuckin' crazy thing just came up here, busted through the front doors. I think it was a bear or some shit. Best get out of here, you know what's good for ya."

Ted showed him the bat. "I got it under control."

He stared at Ted wide-eyed. "Mister, that ain't gonna do a goddamn thing except piss it off."

Ted shrugged and headed toward the On the Run. The alarm increased in volume as he stepped through the shattered entrance. The store was mostly dark inside, save for what little moonlight managed to slip through the windows. Justin had already trashed the place. Aisles of snack foods had collapsed. Dozens of two-liter pops spun on the floor, spitting out foam like rodents cursed with rabies.

The scream of the dying drowned out the store's alarm system. Justin, on the floor, writhing amongst the snack cakes and candy bars and carbonated beverages. His skeletal structure had somehow transformed, returned to a more human-like resemblance. Thick patches of fur covered his skin. Half of his face looked almost human, while the other half looked like dog shit. Bubbles of blood had replaced his eyeballs.

No longer a werewolf, but still not quite a man.

Something in-between.

Ted raised the baseball bat with all intentions of bashing in his friend's skull, then Justin spoke.

"HOLY FUCKING SHIT WHAT THE FUCK SHIT JESUS FUCKING MOTHERFUCK OH MY GOD-DAMN SHIT WHAT THE HELL?"

Ted dropped the bat and backed away, afraid to accidentally bump into him.

"I CAN'T SEE. WHY CAN'T I SEE? WHAT THE FUCK HAPPENED TO ME? OH MY GOD. OH MY FUCKING GOD."

Ted cleared his throat. "I'm here, Justin. It's me."

Justin stopped convulsing and directed his eyeless gaze toward the sound of his voice. "Teddy?"

"Yeah, man."

"What...what happened? Oh goddamn, I hurt all over. Holy shit. Where am I?"

"You got hit by a train."

"A *train?*"

"Yeah."

Justin didn't respond right away, and Ted was sure he'd passed on, then he burst out laughing. "Man, I fuckin' suck at being a werewolf."

And Ted couldn't help but also laugh. Blood spat out of his mouth, which only made him laugh harder. "Yeah, you're pretty terrible at it."

Justin tried to sit up and barely made it an inch off the ground before surrendering back to the floor. "I'm blind, Teddy. I can't see a goddamn thing."

"Yeah. I know."

"Train?"

"I had to stab you."

"In the *eye?*"

Ted nodded, then remembered Justin couldn't see him. "Yeah. In the eye."

"Jesus. With *what?*"

"A fork."

"A *fork?*"

"Yeah."

"Oh, you fucking dick."

"I'm sorry."

Ted limped to the wall cooler and pulled out two tall cans of PBR, then collapsed on the floor next to Justin. Exhaustion had at last won. If the building were to be set ablaze, he would not have the energy to flee. This was a different type of tiredness altogether, something Ted had never quite experienced before. He didn't feel *sleepy*. He felt...*done*. Finished. Past his date of expiration.

"Where the hell we at, anyway?"

"Gas station down the street."

"Weird."

"You want a beer?"

"My fuckin' arms are broken, man."

"Open up."

Ted popped the tab on one of the PBRs and sloshed some down Justin's half-deformed mouth. He choked on it some and let the rest run down the side of his cheek.

"Can't even drink a goddamn beer. What fuckin' good am I?"

"Not much." Ted drank the rest of the can in one long gulp, then threw it across the store. He eyed the other can, still unopened, and threw that one too.

"Hey. How come I ain't dead?"

"Shot you in the head instead of the heart."

Justin chuckled. It sounded disgusting. "I gave you one goddamn direction. Even drew you a little target and everything."

"Guess I was distracted, seeing my wife's severed head in your freezer and all."

A long pause. "Yeah. Sorry about that, Teddy."

Another long pause. "Eh. It's cool."

Outside, the parking lot lit up red and blue.

"Them cops I hear?"

Ted didn't answer. Instead he squeezed his eyes shut so he could be just as blind as Justin.

"Teddy? You still with me, brother?"

"Yeah."

"What happens now?"

"If I had to guess, I'd say we're about to die."

"We?"

"Yeah."

"My doing?"

"Yeah."

"Fuck."

"I would have died eventually, anyway."

"That's a good point." Justin coughed up blood. "Teddy? I'm sorry this all happened, you know. Really. I screwed everything up. I... I love you, man. You know? I fuckin' love you."

Ted reached out with his good hand and patted him on the chest. "I love you, too."

A long silence, and Ted was sure Justin had finally died, only to be proven wrong yet again by another fit of laughter.

"Jesus Christ, what's so funny now?"

A bubble of blood popped out of Justin's mouth as he answered:

"That was super gay, wasn't it?"

Ted grinned. "Yeah. It kind of was."

AUTHOR'S NOTE

This book probably wouldn't exist if Eryk Pruitt hadn't invited me to read at The Wild Detectives in Dallas, TX, on November 12, 2015. The event was called Noir at the Bar, an ongoing reading series involving crime writers preaching their gritty souls to the world. Along with Eryk and myself, this night also witnessed readings from Harry Hunsicker, Rod Davis, Opalina Salas, Scott Montgomery, Jedidiah Ayres, and the great Joe Lansdale. It was the first reading I'd ever participated in, and I couldn't have been more thrilled. Somewhere in the audience sat a man named Will Evans, who would soon go on to form a company called Cinestate with a film producer named Dallas Sonnier (although, Will would leave the company a couple years later). Apparently Will liked what I read, and later reached out to me asking if I had any books I'd like to submit for their new company. I didn't, but that didn't stop me from pitching about half a dozen vague ideas. Eventually we settled on this weird werewolf comedy I'd been thinking about off and on for the past couple months, and I got to work.

Now the book is out, not just through Cinestate but also through motherfucking *FANGORIA*. It's a cliché to say it, I know, but it's true: this a dream come true. Any horror fan worth their salt grew up obsessed with Fangoria, and to have my novel out with them? Holy shit, folks. It doesn't get any cooler than this.

So, thank you, Eryk Pruitt, for giving me that extra push when my anxiety tried its hardest to keep me home, to not make the five-hour drive to Dallas and read in front of a massive crowd of strangers. And thank you, Will Evans, for reaching out and listening to my ideas and saying, I quote: "HOLY FUCKING SHIT MAX THIS IS INSANE AND BRILLIANT!!!!!!!!"

Further appreciation must be directed toward the following:

Betty Rocksteady and Thomas Joyce, for reading early drafts of this manuscript and offering advice to help it not suck.

Josh Malerman, for doing all the things that make him Josh Malerman.

Justin Kattar, for getting drunk with me at work every night as I wrote this novel between 11PM and 7AM.

Dallas Sonnier, Jessica Safavimehr, Preston Fassel, Natasha Pascetta, Ashley Detmering and everybody else doing kickass work at Cinestate, for believing in *CLA* and wanting to take this ride with me.

My mom and dad, for sometimes buying me the new *FANGORIA* after I begged them over and over whenever we went to the grocery store.

And Lori, for everything, always and forever.

ABOUT THE AUTHOR

Raised in Northern Indiana on an unhealthy diet of horror movies and Christopher Pike paperbacks, Max Booth III now lives in San Antonio, TX, where he is constantly trying not to get shot. It is harder than you think. He regularly contributes nonfiction to websites like LitReactor and CrimeReads. He is also the Editor-in-Chief of Perpetual Motion Machine, the Managing Editor of *Dark Moon Digest*, and the co-host of *Castle Rock Radio: A Stephen King Podcast*. Visit his website TalesFromTheBooth.com to learn more and follow him on Twitter @GiveMeYourTeeth.

Carnivorous Lunar Activities is his fifth novel.

CPSIA information can be obtained
at www.ICGtesting.com
Printed in the USA
LVHW090243230119
604833LV00008B/27/P